PN

The Fall
of a
Sparrow

Also by Griselda Heppel

Ante's Inferno

The Tragickall History of Henry Fowst

GRISELDA HEPPEL

The Fall
of a
Sparrow

Wood engraving for cover by Hilary Paynter
Cover design by Pete Lawrence

Matador
9 Priory Business Park,
Wistow Road, Kibworth Beauchamp,
Leicestershire. LE8 0RX
Tel: 0116 279 2299
Email: books@troubador.co.uk
Web: www.troubador.co.uk/matador
Twitter: @matadorbooks

ISBN 978 1800462 502

British Library Cataloguing in Publication Data.
A catalogue record for this book is available from the British Library.

Printed and bound in the UK by TJ Books Limited, Padstow, Cornwall
Typeset in 12pt Aldine401 BT Roman by Troubador Publishing Ltd, Leicester, UK

Matador is an imprint of Troubador Publishing Ltd

In memory of
Rupert Heppel
1950 – 2018

There's a special providence in the fall of a sparrow.
William Shakespeare, *Hamlet*

CHAPTER ONE

One Fine Day in April 1968

They were up to something.

Storming into the kitchen to tell Mum that if Robbie didn't stop doing the twist in front of the TV screen *right now* I'd twist his head right off, I was brought up short. It was something in the way Mum's gaze met mine before dropping back to the sheet of paper on the table before her, the tiny movement of her hand as if she thought to hide it; while Dad just stood, hands in his pockets, looking nowhere in particular.

'What's this?' I said. 'What's going on?'

'Come and sit down, Eleanor,' said Mum. 'We've got something to tell you.'

Oh no. This didn't look good. Sliding into a chair, I glanced at Dad. But he'd seized the kettle, as if this was the most important thing he could do, and was filling it at the sink. On the worktop beside him lay a tray with teapot, cups and saucers, and – what, on a weekday? – a plate of chocolate biscuits. Something was definitely going on.

'Such good news,' said Mum, giving me her most

encouraging smile. 'We've found you a school!'

From the hob the kettle made a rushing sound. I let it fill my brain, willing it to block out the meaning of what I'd just heard. 'I don't need a school,' I said. 'I've got one.'

'No, Eleanor. Things... have changed.' Mum followed Dad with her eyes as he filled the teapot, brought the tray to the table and sat down.

'Proper tea! Shall I call Robbie?' I was already half out of my chair. Anything to derail a conversation that didn't bode well. Even if it meant luring my wretched brother away from his sole mastery of *Crackerjack* on BBC 1 to demolish all the biscuits.

'No.' Dad put a hand on my arm. 'Not yet. Listen to Mum. She's had a letter from your Great-Aunt Margaret, who runs a really nice school in the countryside, in a beautiful old house surrounded by fields and woods and... oh yes.' His eyes gleamed in the way they always did when he tried to enthuse me and Robbie for yet another slog around a mediaeval castle. 'With *ponies*! Doesn't that sound fun?'

I watched Mum pour the tea and couldn't reply.

'The thing is, Ellie—'

'Isn't it wonderful?' Mum snatched up the letter. 'She's offered you a place! For next term! At such short notice I never imagined—'

'*What?*' My hand knocked my cup, splashing tea into the saucer. 'Straight after Easter? No. I'm not going. I'm not leaving West Hill. I'll—'

'Eleanor—'

'—manage better after the holidays, you'll see. I've got Angie' – my voice rose, and I couldn't help it because all the time I talked, Mum just shook her head, her mouth getting tighter and tighter – 'and… and some of the others, they'll be on my side—'

'Mrs Scott phoned last week.'

That silenced me.

'We didn't tell you,' Mum went on. 'Didn't want to upset you, not until we had a solution. She was very calm… and quite pleasant, really… but firm. Said it was regrettable but after what… happened' – Mum's voice went funny, as if the words didn't want to come out – 'she couldn't possibly have you back. I'm sorry, darling.'

'Not have me…' I got no further. Everything – blue and white crockery, scrubbed pine tabletop, Mum's hand holding the letter – dissolved into a blur in which images from that last awful day flooded my mind and wouldn't disappear, no matter how hard I blinked.

Mum put down the letter. 'Eleanor, listen,' she said. 'It may be for the best.'

Now my head shot up. 'How can it be for the best? I've been expelled! How fair is that?'

I knew something had to happen, that there'd be… what was Mrs Scott's favourite word? Ah yes, *consequences*. They'd been hanging over me all through the holidays, she'd made sure of that. But this!

'Not expelled.' Dad put his arm around my shoulders. 'You've been asked to leave. That's different. No one at your next school need know your record.'

I yanked my shoulder away. 'My... I have a *record*?'

Mum glanced at the door but luckily the kids' cheering on *Crackerjack* covered everything else. 'Of course you haven't.' She glared at Dad. 'But you do need a fresh start. And that's where Great-Aunt Margaret comes in. I wrote to her, you see, as soon as we knew... the state of things... and she replied at once. A good sign, don't you see? She really wants you!'

Rubbing my face on my sleeve, I tried to focus on her, tried to take in the meaning behind that eager smile. 'How can she want me?' I said at last. 'I've never met her, never even heard of her. Who is Great-Aunt Margaret?'

'Great-Aunt Margaret—' Mum began.

Then it hit me. *Nice school in the countryside*, Dad had described it, *with fields, woods, ponies*... A hollow opened up in my stomach. 'Oh no,' I said. 'It's a boarding school, isn't it? You're sending me away.'

No need for either of them to answer. Not when their expressions said it all.

'I can't believe this,' I said. 'You want to get rid of me too, just like Mrs Scott.'

'Eleanor, *no*.' Mum's face crumpled. 'Of course we don't. But we tried all the schools around here. None of them had room.'

I stared at her. So that's what all those 'work' phone calls last week had been about, for which she'd shooed Robbie and me into the garden so she could concentrate. The floor seemed to slide from under my feet and I wrapped my ankles around the legs of my chair, pressing my bones hard against the wood. 'Not true,' I said. 'There must be somewhere.'

Dad shook his head. 'I'm afraid n—'

'There *must* be.' I wouldn't look at him. Or Mum. '*Some* school that will... yes!' It came to me. 'What about St Chad's? I could go there with Mum and Robbie! OK, so they don't normally take girls, but—'

It was no use.

'I know this sounds hard,' said Dad, putting his hand on mine, 'but Mum and I think it will be good for you to get away completely. And Ashstone House is an excellent school.'

'You can learn to ride, Eleanor!' Mum's eyes shone. 'You've always wanted to do that. Now's your chance.'

My leg muscles began to ache as a wave of tiredness swept through me. Unwrapping my ankles from the chair legs, I sat up and took a few sips of tea. To my surprise there flickered, somewhere deep inside me, the tiniest spark. It was true. I *had* always wanted to ride. Ever since watching *Champion the Wonder Horse*, anyway. Just like Robbie wanted to drive a tank and mow people down.

Coming round the table, Mum gave me a hug. I buried my face in her shoulder, woollen threads

5

tickling my nose, and took a few deep breaths. All right, then. If this was what I had to do, I'd do it. Then the thought came that soon I'd have to manage without hugs like this, and I couldn't speak.

'Right.' Rising to his feet, Dad smoothed down the hair at the back of his head. 'I'm only halfway through redrafting Chapter 8, so...'

'Wait.' Pulling away from Mum, I looked at her. 'You still haven't explained about Great-Aunt Margaret. Why've I never heard of her before?'

'Because,' said Mum, 'I hadn't either, not until five years ago. She wrote to tell me her husband had died. It seems he was my uncle – Grandpa Fielding's brother.'

Now I forgot everything. 'Grandpa had a *brother*?'

The door swung open and Robbie charged in. 'Ha, you missed a smashing programme, El – hey!' His eyes fell on the table. 'Chocolate biscuits! Why didn't anyone tell me?'

CHAPTER TWO

Ashstone House

For the next two weeks, the happiest person in our household was, without a doubt, Robbie. While I woke every morning with butterflies in my stomach at the thought that, not today, no, but soon, everything in my life was about to change, Robbie took to entering my room and looking round, as if deciding which part to occupy first. I threw him out, of course, so then he made for the sitting room to bounce on the sofa, crowing that now, at last, he'd get to watch whatever he wanted on television; and, seeing as I wasn't going to be around, he might as well have my after-lunch sweet ration too. When, on the last day of the holidays, he interrupted my packing every ten minutes to tell me what time it was, even Angie – who'd come over to see me off – rolled her eyes.

'Guess there are some people round here you won't miss that much,' she murmured.

Crouching down to rifle through my bookcase for which of my favourites to take, I had my back to the room. 'I'll miss you,' I said.

'Ah – hum. Me too,' she said. 'But you'll make lots of new friends, don't worry. Ashstone House sounds so cool.'

'Yeah.' I stared at the books in front of me.

'And the head being your long-lost relation!' Angie flopped onto my bed. 'I still can't believe nobody knew about her. Not even your mum.'

'Yup.' Rising, I tossed a couple of paperbacks into my trunk lying open on the floor. 'A family rift, apparently. Happened long before Mum was even born. She grew up thinking her father was an only child.'

'That's so sad.' Angie folded her arms over her knees. 'Do you think they had an argument, your great-uncle and your grandpa?'

'Who knows?' I shrugged. The figure of the grandpa I could only just remember rose before me: a tall, shadowy presence with watery eyes and a soft moustache, who patted my five-year-old head and hid jelly babies in my pockets. How could anyone pick a fight with him?

A thundering on the door followed by a piercing, 'At the *next* stroke, it will be 11.30 am pre*cisely*,' made us both jump. Angie's head hit the wall behind her, and her face screwed up in pain. That was when it occurred to me that picking a fight with your brother might not be so unlikely after all.

Robbie knew what he was doing, though. If I could have stopped time passing, I would have. I closed my trunk, chatted away to Angie, tried to eat lunch, anything not to think about the moment when Dad would finish packing up the Mini and that would be that. But at last I couldn't duck it anymore. As Dad held the passenger door open for me to climb through into the back, I turned to say goodbye to Angie and Robbie – and for a second wondered where my brother had got to.

''Bye, Ellie.' Angie gave me a big smile. 'Good luck!'

Returning the smile with the broadest one I could manage, I spotted Robbie, and realised why I hadn't before. He wasn't leaping about. Or crowing. He just stood beside Mrs Stewart from next door who'd come over to look after him, saying nothing, one hand clutching something in his pocket, watching as first I, then Mum, got into the car.

Then, as we were about to leave, Robbie dashed forward, a funny, solemn expression on his face, and thrust his arm around the frame of Mum's open window. I felt something drop into my lap, but Dad started the engine and I just had time to wave at Robbie as we drove off.

It wasn't until we'd left them all behind that I looked to see what he'd given me.

Loki, his favourite troll.

I held it tight for a long time, stroking its long, straggly black hair.

The drive took hours. Ashstone House lay deep in the Dorset countryside, and the roads wound more and more, so that by the time we descended a long track leading to a great, square, gabled house, I was too sick to care what came next. After a minute or two of gulping the fresh air outside the car, I followed Mum and Dad down a dark stone porch to an open door at the end, where a figure waited to greet us.

'Frances, James – how lovely to meet you.'

As Mum and Dad leaned forwards to shake hands, I caught a glimpse of a stately, white-haired lady with a hook nose and pale eyes. Turning, she led the way along one side of a huge, square hall, filled with long tables laid for supper.

'This is so good of you, Aunt Margaret,' said Mum. 'I don't know what we'd have done without—'

The white curls fluttered, showing a bluish tinge, as the figure walking before me shook her head. 'Don't, please.' She raised her hand. 'I was so glad you got in touch. I hated this whole business, you know. I could never understand Alexander's attitude. I'd have got him and your father together long ago if I'd had my way. I expect you felt the same.' Reaching a staircase, she turned right down a dark corridor.

'Well, yes.' Mum hurried to catch up. 'I would have if—'

'Ah. You didn't know about it, I forgot. Better that way, perhaps.'

'Actually—' Mum began.

'Come in, come in!' Throwing open a door, my great-aunt ushered us through it. 'Sit down and tell me all about yourselves.' Waving my parents to a worn, pale blue sofa near a big marble fireplace, she turned to me. 'And now, Eleanor, let's have a look…'

She stopped dead. The warmth in her expression vanished, to be replaced by something that looked like shock. It certainly shocked me. I stood, hardly daring to breathe, as she stared at me, motionless, save for a slight quivering around her chin; and when at last she moved to sit down opposite my parents, I almost fell back, as if released by a spring. As Mum leaned forwards, eager for family information – which, judging by the closed look that now appeared on my great-aunt's face, she was getting very little of – and Dad nodded at intervals, as if that could disguise the way his gaze, as ever, slid around all the architectural details of the room, I stayed where I was, puzzling over that stare. What could it mean? Was I so different from expected?

I was still trying to work it out when my great-aunt rose to her feet. 'Right,' she said. 'Time to show Eleanor where she'll be sleeping. All she needs for now is her overnight bag; trunks will be brought up in the morning.'

I stood up straight, ready to smile, but she swept past without a look. Instead, Mum put her arm round me as we followed my great-aunt out of her study and up the wide, polished oak staircase. Turning left at the top brought us into a gloomy room lit by sash windows on one side, in which four beds covered in identical yellow bedspreads, and a single painting of flowers in a blue jug on the wall, gave the only splashes of colour.

Looking round at all that heavy, dark furniture and wooden panelling, I felt something shrivel inside me.

My great-aunt must have noticed because her voice took on a cheery note. 'Fairfax won't look deserted for long, you'll see. By this evening it'll be mayhem in here.' She cast her gaze heavenward as if in need of help. 'Down there' – she pointed through a doorway straight opposite – 'is Hampden, for the little ones; then the bathroom, and my bedroom round the corner. If anyone gets up to mischief during the night I know about it. Nothing gets past me.'

Mum smiled nervously, trying to catch my eye; which was more than I could say for my great-aunt. She'd still not so much as glanced my way. It was almost as if, having seen my face once, she couldn't bear to do so again. But why? What had I done?

Of course. She knew. *It was Mrs Scott, I bet it was!* All that stuff she told Mum about no one at my next school needing to know... Had she been lying? If so – my hands clenched into fists by my sides – if ever I got back to West Hill and set eyes on that pinch-nosed, tight-lipped hypocrite of a headmistress again, I'd... I'd...

'Eleanor,' said Mum, 'are you all right?'

I nodded, unclenching my fists.

'The term will fly by, you'll see,' said Dad. 'My goodness, what a splendid house. Fairfax, Hampden – I love the idea of naming all the dormitories after Civil War generals. And, Ellie, look at this.' Walking over to a small diamond-patterned window, he reached for the handle. 'Funny to have windows overlooking the dining room, isn't it? It's because it was originally an open courtyard before someone thought of covering it with a glass lantern. Much later, of course. Come and see.'

Poking my head out, I followed his gaze upwards to the thick, misty panes above.

'From the second floor you should be able to get out onto the roof and walk round the glass bit. You'd have to keep to the leads, of course – you know, the flat parts – but that wouldn't be diffic—'

'James,' said Mum, 'do you mind switching work off just for once? Ashstone House is not one of your research projects.'

From the sash window at the opposite end of the room, where she'd been showing Mum the view, Great-Aunt Margaret crossed the floor and pulled the casement closed. 'These are never opened, James. We don't want anyone leaning out. And there is certainly no access to the roof from the top floor.'

'Oh. Ah, of course. Sorry.' Reddening, Dad fell back and ran his eyes around the ceiling, as if seeking refuge in one of the corners.

His confusion made me smile. But not for long.

A clattering came from the staircase outside. Someone was stamping the whole way up, talking loudly to the person behind her. '…don't care what you say, Dad, I can't believe I'm in Fairfax *again*.'

'Ah, Eleanor,' said my great-aunt. 'Here comes your first room-mate.'

CHAPTER THREE

Lorna

A girl with long flick-back hair and a disgusted look in her eyes marched in. Behind her, a man with a very pink, very smooth head carried in one hand a small leather case and in the other an enormous Gonk cuddly toy with purple psychedelic trousers and green hair.

Seeing the headmistress, the girl made straight for her. 'Mrs Fielding, I thought I'd be in Grange this term? With Nina?'

'Hello, Lorna,' said my great-aunt. 'You know perfectly well that no one goes into Grange until after her twelfth birthday. Grange' – she turned to Mum and Dad – 'is for the older girls. It's run by my daughter and her husband, and everyone imagines they'll have more fun there, I can't think why. Because not even you, Lorna' – a gleam came into her eye – 'would make the mistake of taking Mr and Mrs Lockwood to be a soft touch. Now, come and meet Eleanor. I want you to show her round.'

'Told you, silly,' said the pink man. 'Hello, Mrs Fielding. By the window again, Lorna?' With a nod to us, he made for the left-hand bed and plonked suitcase and Gonk on top of it.

Lorna made no move. 'So is Nina in Fairfax too?' she demanded.

'The other two girls are Lucy Richards and Susanna Phiri. Nina Coates is in Verney, not a million miles away. You two can't always be together, not when there are others to think about.'

That's when Lorna looked at me. *So you're the reason*, said her eyes.

'Now,' said my great-aunt, 'time for goodbyes. Best let the girls get on with it.'

'Goodbye, darling.' Mum put her arms around me. 'See you very soon.'

'Roll on the weekend after next,' said Dad, giving me a hug. 'It'll be here before we know it.'

I couldn't return his hug. The weekend after next – the earliest we'd be allowed out – felt light years away. I stared unblinking at my great-aunt's – Mrs Fielding's – back as she ushered them out, until all I could see was a smudge of blue-white hair on top of a mauve cardigan.

'You coming or not?'

Swallowing, I turned to see Lorna in the opposite doorway. I nodded.

Striding down the corridor, she pointed to a closed door on the left. 'Hampden. Where the squits sleep.'

Squits? They sounded like some sort of watery vegetables, like marrows. I imagined them all tucked up in their beds, fatter ends resting on pillows.

Reaching the bathroom at the end of the corridor, Lorna turned in the doorway. 'Do you have a pony?'

'No,' I said. 'I can't ride. But' – and the picture rose before me of the one glorious thing this new school offered – 'I can't wait to learn.'

The right answer, judging by Lorna's quick nod. 'I've got a pony,' she said. 'He's called Domino. Because he's black with four white socks and a blaze.'

'Ablaze? You mean he's on fire?'

'Ha ha, very funny. OK, so this is the bathroom.'

I managed to peep round her, glimpsing several shower cubicles and basins, white islands rising out of a blue floor, before she pushed me back into the corridor.

'Domino's only just over twelve hands,' she said. 'So he'll be too small for me soon, which is awful because I adore him. Hey, where are you going?'

I'd assumed we'd be following the corridor round, and had turned the corner. Though I have to admit the darkness made me waver.

'Not that way,' said Lorna. 'Mrs Fielding's bedroom is down there, and Chloe's and… some other things. We're not allowed past the bathroom.'

'Who's Chloe?' I asked. 'And what other things?'

Ahead on both sides, door frames jutted into the gloom. The nearest one on the left lay dark, but from the next one along came an electric glow and the low murmur of a radio. Beyond, the passage stretched into a blackness so deep you could almost touch it.

'Oh, you'll find out.' Tossing back her hair, Lorna retraced her steps to Fairfax.

I turned to follow – and froze. A sound had split the darkness behind me. Something like a gasp – of delight? Surprise? I spun round.

Nothing. As my eyes adjusted to the dimness, I could see where, far down the corridor, a pale light trickled in. From the sound of distant footsteps and voices, girls were arriving on that side of the house too.

I let out a long breath. A trick of the dark, nothing more. Someone down there had just shouted a greeting to a friend, and somehow my brain misinterpreted it as being close by.

On the back of my neck, even.

With a shiver I clutched the points of my shirt collar close and headed back to Fairfax.

'Oh, there you are, Eleanor,' said Lorna. 'This is Lucy.'

A girl with tight copper curls gave me a smile. 'Hello, El—'

'Wait.' Lorna looked at me. 'Are you anything for short? Like—'

Here it comes, I thought. But I was prepared. 'No.'

'—Ellie?'

'No!' I'd said no, hadn't I? 'I'm Eleanor. Just Eleanor, OK?'

'O… K.' Lorna's voice went up and down as her eyes met Lucy's.

'Hello, *Eleanor*,' said Lucy, putting her head on one

17

side. 'Don't worry, I understand.' She nodded several times, just to make sure I got the message.

I felt about four years old.

'So, Lorna's been showing you round.' Tactfully, Lucy changed the subject. 'Did she tell you about the Huntsman?'

'What huntsman?'

Lorna rolled her eyes. 'There's an old loo down the corridor, past Mrs Fielding's bedroom, and it's supposed to be haunted by the ghost of a huntsman—'

'*Supposed* to be?' Lucy gave me a large wink.

'—with a broken leg, and the moment you shut the door he appears from the shadows, dragging his leg, and—'

'Stop!' said Lucy. 'You'll frighten Eleanor.'

Did she see something in my face? That strange sensation I'd had in the corridor crept over my skin, and I shook it away. What I'd heard sounded nothing like a man dragging a broken leg. 'I'm OK,' I said.

After that, Lorna had no more time for me. And something in the way Lucy held her head and busied herself around Lorna told me that Lorna's having time for her came as a delightful surprise. Together they set about unpacking, Lucy having taken the bed next to Lorna's, and their bedside tables – which, close to, turned out to be old wooden boxes, painted and stood on their ends – quickly filled up. Lorna's held – barely – a beige plastic horse, nearly a foot high, complete with plastic saddle, bridle and other pieces of equipment.

Lucy's also boasted a horse, but much smaller, dark brown and made of china. Taking the bed opposite Lorna, I stowed my hairbrush, torch, alarm clock and book on the slatted shelf inside the bedside box and, smoothing down his straggly hair, placed Loki on top. OK, so he wasn't a horse, but his cheeky smile more than made up for that.

One bed remained empty. 'Susanna,' said Lorna. 'Don't worry about her. She's always late.'

'Does she have far to come?' I asked.

'You could say that.' Lorna gave a small smile.

I wondered why.

CHAPTER FOUR

Susanna

And then of course Susanna arrived, and I made a complete fool of myself. Well, why wouldn't I think she'd flown direct from Africa? Susanna herself didn't mind. I wasn't to know she'd lived in London for the past four years, ever since her family had left Malawi. Giving me a smile, she threw herself down on the bed next to mine, her thick black hair bouncing in tight bunches either side of her head. I couldn't help grinning back.

'Because she'd never have got here in one day,' said Lorna. 'Not your strong point, geography, is it, Eleanor?'

Lucy smiled in a we-shouldn't-be-too-hard-on-her way, which made me want to clock her one even more than Lorna. Turning my back, I concentrated on Susanna unpacking her overnight bag, waiting to see if she too would place a horse on her box. Instead, a smooth, hand-carved giraffe appeared, all dark wood and light wood for its patterned coat, and beside it, a honey-coloured lion. I helped her balance them – the lion's outstretched paws were particularly tricky.

'They're lovely,' I said. 'From Malawi?'

She nodded. 'They remind me. This, too.' On her knee she held a battered-looking calendar. Carefully turning the pages to April, she propped it up on the shelf inside her box.

I crouched down on my heels to see the picture: a deep blue lake with grassland beyond, and in the distance, mountains under heavy, overhanging clouds. 'Susanna,' I said, 'this is for 1964.'

'Yes.'

'But that's—'

'Four years ago. I know. When we left.' She stayed looking down at the shelf for a moment. The corners of her mouth drooped.

'I'm sorry.' I couldn't think what else to say.

She shrugged. 'It's OK. One day we'll go back.' She nodded firmly, though her eyes said something else.

'Hurry up!' From the doorway came Mrs Fielding's voice. 'You girls should be in your pyjamas by now.'

Twisting round, I stayed where I was, close to the floor. Was I seeing things? Earlier, in my great-aunt's study, transfixed by that chilly stare, the wild thought came to me that with her hook nose and bushy white hair, all that was missing was a broomstick in her hand… and now this! While she bustled through the dorm, making eye contact with everyone but me, I stood up slowly, watching the other girls. None looked the least bothered that their headmistress was clearly a witch.

'Susanna,' I said, the moment we were on our own again, 'was that a – a *raven* on her shoulder?'

Susanna snorted. 'Not quite. It's a jackdaw.'

'Why on earth—'

'Beaky's a pet,' said Lucy. 'Birds can be pets, you know, Eleanor.'

Of course I knew. Biting my lip, I looked away, the picture still fresh in my mind of a small, hooded, jet-black head swivelling round to fix me with one pale eye.

A quarter of an hour's reading time, and then – much too early, from the pale crack between the curtains – lights out. While Lorna and Lucy whispered opposite, I lay open-eyed, staring at the ceiling. Snapshots of the last few hours jostled in my head, always coming to rest on the figure of my great-aunt, breaking off her friendly greeting to stand speechless, as still as stone, the instant she laid eyes on me. What was that about? It looked as if, having encouraged me to come here, the moment I appeared she changed her mind. Couldn't bear the sight of me, in fact. But why? Did she suddenly remember my… my *record*, and decide she wanted nothing to do with me?

Turning, I pressed my face into the pillow. Too bad. I was here now. Perhaps she just feared I'd use our relationship to lord it over the other girls – as if I would! – and this was her way of making sure I didn't. Well, she needn't have worried. If she didn't want to be acknowledged, didn't want to be called 'Great-Aunt

Margaret', that was fine by me. 'Mrs Fielding' was much less of a mouthful.

We were woken the next morning by a handbell rung by a brisk woman with short, wiry black hair and bright eyes that made me think of a fox terrier. While the headmistress took charge of putting us to bed, it was Miss Stalkland – the matron – who made sure we leapt out again in the morning. Dressing quickly, we joined the rush down to breakfast in the hall, where we sat down on the long benches and began to pass round plates of bread and bowls of marmalade.

That's when a strange thing happened.

A tall, thin lady with long, slow-moving limbs placed herself opposite me. That in itself was odd. Only girls sat on the benches. Grown-ups were meant to sit on chairs at the ends of the tables, instead of having to slide their legs between table and bench, as this lady was doing now. Straightening up, she ate her breakfast slowly, eyes down, not speaking to any of the chattering, wriggling girls around her. It worked both ways since, apart from being careful to pass her plates of food, the girls on either side ignored the lady completely.

Yet I couldn't take my eyes off her. She was just… beautiful. I didn't think you could be when you were that old (she must have been thirty-five at least), but she had lovely clear skin, and smooth dark hair, pulled back from her brow and held in a clasp at the nape of her neck. After breakfast, she drifted away towards the stairs and I asked Lorna which teacher she was.

'*Teacher?*' said Lorna. 'That's no teacher. That's just Chloe.'

'Oh, but she does teach a bit,' said Lucy, as we made our way back up to the dorm. 'She does art with the little ones.'

'Hardly,' Lorna snorted. 'The squits only have her because Mrs Fielding's too scary for them. Chloe just wanders around the art room looking vague and they do what they like. We used to go wild.'

'So why is she here?' I asked. 'And why does she sit with us?'

'She's here because she's Mrs Fielding's daughter, Mrs Lockwood's sister,' said Lucy. 'And where do you expect her to sit? Not at the end of the table. She couldn't possibly keep order. I'd have thought that was obvious, Eleanor.'

There was a brief moment at the top of the stairs when I longed for Lucy to trip over the threshold of Fairfax and go flying. The temptation flickered to reveal that, actually, both Chloe and Mrs Lockwood were cousins of mine... but it passed. Going down that path would demand explanations I didn't want to give.

Maybe Lucy felt bad for putting me down, because she then became extra nice all that first day, sitting next to me in the classroom, showing me which books I'd be using. All I had was a pencil case, and my desk felt empty; until a shadow fell across it and I glanced up to see a tall girl with long, wavy chestnut hair.

'So,' she said, 'you're the reason I'm in Verney, not Fairfax. Nice to meet you, new girl.' She gave me a smile that wasn't a smile, not with the way her mouth turned down at the corners.

A knot lodged itself in my stomach. 'H-hello,' I said. 'Sorry.'

Lucy finished returning the books to her desk and snapped the lid shut. 'Don't blame Eleanor, Nina,' she said.

'Yeah,' came Susanna's voice from behind. 'It's not her fault.'

'Whoa.' Nina put up her hands. 'Did I say it was?' Sauntering away, she sat down at a desk on the far side of Lorna.

'Thanks,' I mumbled.

Stretched out in her chair, twirling a lock of hair around her finger, Susanna winked at me.

'It's fine,' said Lucy. But her gaze slid towards where Lorna and Nina now leaned, heads together, whispering, as if she regretted not being part of their conversation. Being Lorna's best friend in the dorm didn't, it seemed, count for much outside it.

The day passed in a whirl of lessons and breaks spent mostly bouncing balls on the playground next to the classrooms. At lunchtime we lined up to enter the dining hall by a big archway on the opposite side from the main entrance. Craning my neck to see past the people in front, I blinked as shafts of light pierced the glass panes above to glance off tumblers and cutlery.

As the queue began to move, Susanna pulled me to one side and pointed to a noticeboard. 'That's you, isn't it?' she said. 'I didn't know you play the piano.'

'What?' I squinted over the heads of other girls who stopped to check the freshly typed notice pinned to the board. 'Oh, it's a timetable.' I spotted my name written into the last morning lesson space the next day. 'Yes, that's me.'

'Looks like you'll be missing English tomorrow,' said Susanna. 'Don't worry, I'll tell Mrs Lockwood you've got a piano lesson. Now,' she added, leading the way into the dining room, 'try to get a seat on the far side of your table, along the wall. That way, if it's stewed prunes, you can tip them behind the radiator and no one'll know.'

CHAPTER FIVE

The Boy in the Mirror

Thanks to Susanna's instructions, I found the music room with time to spare. Dropping my music case by the piano, I hovered there for a moment, taking in the warm, peppery smell of polished floorboards, before wandering over to look at the great gilt-framed mirror over the fireplace. Leaning my elbows on the mantelpiece, I glanced at my reflection, only to jerk back as something in the glass above caught my eye.

A boy stood there. Or rather, he was jumping up and down, shaking his hands fast in a funny way, and when our eyes met in the mirror he broke into the biggest smile I'd ever seen. He had fair hair, so fair it was almost white, and wore a grey short-sleeved shirt and dark grey shorts down to his knees, which had a muddy look, though with him jigging up and down it was hard to tell. But the strangest thing of all was his sheer joy at seeing me. 'It *is* you – I knew it!' he cried, with a great gasp of delight. 'I knew it from the first! You're back, you're *back*,' he kept saying, giggling, and flicking his hands so hard he looked in danger of dislocating his wrists.

I turned to face him, questions bubbling up inside, but just then the door opened and a little round-shouldered woman entered, carrying some music under her arm. Giving me a smile, she said, 'Ah – you must be Eleanor. I'm Mrs Turner.' When I looked back, the boy had gone. I didn't hear him opening the door on the far side of the room but he must have slipped through – afraid, perhaps, he'd be told off for disturbing a music lesson.

For the next half-hour I tried to play my piano pieces, but I just couldn't get the boy out of my head. Who was he? What was he doing in a girls' boarding school? Perhaps Mrs Fielding had a grandson. That would make us second (or third?) cousins – but since our families had never met, nor even known about each other, how could he be so pleased to see me? And yet there was something familiar about him. Not so much in what he looked like, more in what he…

My hands slipped off the keys onto the wood of the piano.

'Don't stop,' said Mrs Turner. 'You were doing fine.'

'Sorry.' Fixing my eyes on the music, I forced my fingers to move against the cold, stiff feeling that had taken hold of them.

That sound. That gasp of delight. I'd heard it before.

I shook the thought from my head. Coincidence, nothing more. Somehow, this strange boy's excitement had brought back the odd trick my ears played on me in the corridor that first evening.

When at last the lesson ended, I headed to the dining hall to find Susanna. If anyone could tell me about the boy, she could. But searching the sea of faces as I arrived, my eyes fell not on Susanna, but on Lucy, who happened at that moment to turn and, with a big smile, pat the place beside her.

Well, Lucy would take me seriously, at least.

Once Mrs Fielding had said grace, we all sat down, tucking our legs under the benches, and I told my tale. Lucy listened, head bent forward and eyebrows raised slightly, which had the effect of lengthening her face so that I was sorely tempted to pat her on the nose, as if she were one of the ponies in the stables. When I finished, she stayed in that position, playing with the gold horseshoe on a chain around her neck, and I actually had to sit on both my hands while I waited for her answer.

'It must have been the Lockwoods' son,' she said. 'David. He's about six, I think. There's him and his little sister, Alice. Both very fair. Goodness knows what he was doing in the music room. Looking for his grandmother, I suppose.'

'David Lockwood,' I murmured.

So I was right. He was my cousin. Grange, where he must live with his family, stood about fifty yards from the main school, with a single enormous cedar and the chapel in between. A six-year-old could run between the two quite easily. Except that the boy I saw looked older, more like Robbie's age.

'Well, David's quite tall for six,' said Lucy. 'I suppose someone *might* mistake him for a nine-year-old.'

The urge to pat her on the nose turned into something rather stronger, but luckily I needed my hands just then to pass plates of shepherd's pie down the table. I was about to argue that of course I could tell the difference between the two ages, that something here didn't fit; but Lucy started eating so I did too. After all, I thought, through forkfuls of hot, savoury mince and mashed potato, I'd barely laid eyes on this boy before he disappeared. In all that smiling and jiggling up and down, perhaps I did imagine him taller and older than he was.

Yet him being my cousin didn't explain why he'd greeted me with such joy, as if we were old friends. He must have mistaken me for someone else; perhaps a girl who'd been at Ashstone and left. How disappointed he would be when he found out the truth! Next time I saw him, I'd have to tell him, and I was bound to see him again sooner or later.

But as the days passed, I didn't. And people I asked seemed surprised that I knew about him at all.

'David Lockwood?' said Lorna. 'We only see him at chapel on Sunday mornings. Otherwise he's over at Grange with his parents, or at primary school. He'd never be allowed to run around Ashstone on his own, he's much too little. You must've imagined him, Eleanor.'

How could I have imagined someone I didn't even know existed? There had to be some other explanation.

Perhaps he did venture out occasionally, when no one was looking. I determined to watch out for him.

So, that Saturday afternoon, as Lucy and Susanna showed me round the school grounds, I only half listened, keeping an eye out for David. He didn't appear as we climbed the lower branches of the cedar tree by the chapel, nor as we wandered across the games field to the woodland beyond; nor as, later, we doubled back around the front of the house to the playground on the other side to play ball games, until Webster – Mrs Fielding's golden retriever – joined in, and the game turned into a glorious mess of warm fur, dog saliva and laughter.

I forgot about the boy after that as Lucy and Susanna took me to meet the ponies. The stables lay on the far side of the playground and across a yard of soft earth and sawdust churned up by horses' hooves. Stepping inside, I stood for a moment, filling my nostrils with delicious scents of leather, molasses and polish as I waited for my sight to adjust to the half-light. Then I walked with the others between the loose boxes, where smells of urine and dung made my eyes water.

In the first stall, a fat pony with a long, straggly red mane and tail stood with his back to us. 'This is Happy,' said Lucy. 'He's a Shetland. That's why he's so stocky. Beginners usually start on him.' She looked me up and down. 'Not so far to fall.'

I folded my arms to conceal the small jolt that went through me. Fall? Not something I'd reckoned with.

Lucy raised an eyebrow. 'Not scared, are you, Eleanor?'

'No. Not at all. Absolutely not.' I folded my arms the other way, the way that never feels right when you do it and pretty soon you have to do it the first way again. 'I... er...'

'Yes?'

'Oh, you know.' I put my head on one side. 'I was just thinking. All that red and white... not really my colour. Do you have another one in that size, but in black?'

Susanna gave a shout of laughter, sending a quiver of surprise down Happy's neck.

Lucy closed her eyes. 'It's called *skewbald*,' she hissed. 'Not *red* and *white*. For goodness' sake, Eleanor, the sooner you learn about ponies the better for you.'

'Oops. Sorry.' I tried to stop my lips twitching.

Susanna dug me in the ribs. 'You'll be fine,' she whispered. 'But watch out for Happy. He likes biting your ankle when you're mounting him.'

Happy gave me a sidelong glance, as if judging exactly the best part of my leg to sink his teeth into. I backed away.

'Come and meet Magic,' said Susanna. 'You'll like him.'

In the box next door stood a medium-sized black pony with a gleaming coat, just asking to be stroked. So I did, daring to run my hand down his nose this time, right down to the soft, velvety bit around his nostrils.

He let out a long breath, warming my fingers.

'Oh, he's lovely,' I said. 'I love the white stripe down his face.'

Lucy groaned. 'It's called a blaze, Eleanor. Not a stripe. And you see his legs? Those patches of white just above his hooves: they're called socks.'

'Ah,' I said. So that was what Lorna had been talking about that first, bewildering evening.

On Sunday morning we lined up in the dining hall. Above the general chatter came the steady ring of the chapel bell, and the wait until the door to the porch opened seemed to go on forever.

'Don't know why you're so keen to go, Eleanor,' said Lorna. 'The service will be pretty boring.'

'Perhaps she's religious,' said Nina. She gave me her usual unnerving smile, mouth curved the wrong way.

I shook my head, feeling hot prickles on the back of my neck, and tried to look cool. As if I couldn't care less that now at last I'd see Mrs Lockwood's son for myself and be sure, one way or the other, if he was the strange boy from the music room.

It didn't work out that way. When at last we filed through the porch, across the drive and into the old stone building, I ended up in a corner by the organ. Sticking out halfway down the chapel, it blocked my view of most of the pews by the entrance where the teachers sat; and as Mr Lockwood came in, I strained every muscle, willing him to head to his right, the only part of the seating area I could see. Instead, he turned left, standing aside for his wife, who, eyes down, steered the two invisible children in front of her into the pew.

Leaning back, I hit my head against the wall and groaned. Why couldn't they have taken the opposite side? I had a fine view of Mrs Fielding sitting there in the front, in a flowery blouse and smart navy skirt, hair unusually smooth. I waited for her to stand up and take the service, as she did with assembly in the dining hall. Instead, Mr Lockwood, in a less battered tweed jacket than the one he wore for maths lessons, rose to his feet and, with a swift, quelling glance at all of us, announced the first hymn.

As Mrs Turner started to play the organ, a figure in a beige skirt and cream cardigan glided into the seat next to Mrs Fielding. Bending forwards, Mrs Fielding looked as if she wanted to speak, but Chloe never gave her a glance. To my surprise, something about the way Mrs Fielding remained for a moment, head bowed, before slowly getting to her feet, sent a wave of pity through me. Without Beaky on her shoulder, his bright, piercing eyes imitating hers, she looked much older. Frail, even.

At the end of the service, I craned to catch sight of the Lockwoods leaving their pew, but it was hopeless. People crowded in front of me, and by the time I reached the exit there was no sign of Mrs Lockwood or her children; just her husband remained to usher us all back to the house.

It wasn't the end of the world, I told myself. The mystery was bound to solve itself at some point; and even if it didn't, so what? I'd stumbled upon a boy larking around in the music room, that was all. Yet even as I thought of him, that extraordinary light in his eyes rushed back to me with such strength, it was as if I carried him through the rest of the morning. As I sat down in South Hall for letter-writing – our next task before lunch – his figure jumped off the page and I stared for ages at the blank paper, head aching with the effort of thinking of things I could actually write home about, which didn't include a fair-haired boy with muddy knees who giggled and flapped his arms in a strange way.

Beside me, Lucy wrote steady, neat lines. Susanna tapped her pen against her teeth, her gaze fixed far away. Lorna, opposite, had filled two pages already – mainly with stick drawings of horses going over jumps. She must have felt my eyes on her because, without raising her head, she blocked her paper with her arm, as if I were trying to copy off her in a maths test.

Instead, I looked around. South Hall lay on the other side of the dining hall from Ashstone House's main entrance, through the archway where we lined up for lunch. On the walls hung a number of paintings, mainly of vases of flowers, like the one in our dorm. Others showed green meadows with tall daisies swaying in the long grass, or scarlet poppies dotting a hot yellow cornfield. One in particular caught my eye: ancient tree trunks swathed in ivy, sunlight dappling the leaves and falling across a path that curled through bluebells, a shimmer of mauve, pink and white.

'Eleanor.'

I jumped.

'I'm glad you like my sister's paintings,' said Mrs Lockwood, from directly behind me. 'However, a little less art appreciation and a little more letter-writing is what you should be doing right now.'

Lorna and Nina sniggered. Gripping my pen, I drove it across the paper.

> *Dear Mummy and Daddy,*
>   *I hope you are well. I miss you. I can't wait for next weekend when you can come and take me out…*

It was just as well letter-writing took place then. A few hours later and I couldn't have written anything they'd have allowed me to send.

Not after what happened that afternoon.

CHAPTER SIX

Running Free

It was the rain that did it.

For a while Lucy, Susanna and I tried playing ball in the playground. When puddles started forming on the tarmac, we gave up and walked round the house to the cedar, where girls slid off the branches onto wet grass. Finally, as the rain got heavier, we ran across the games field to the wood.

Lorna, Nina and a few others were already there, standing under a huge tree, whose great sheltering branches sprouted leaves so thickly they caught the rain long before it reached the ground. Leaves clustered also around the lower part of the trunk, from a mass of shoots springing from the base. Threading my way around these, I found a clear patch of bark and leaned back against it, closing my eyes. There were worse places to wait out a shower.

After a moment, Lorna spoke. 'Right, the rain's eased off. We can carry on.'

Opening my eyes, I had the strangest feeling. I knew this place. The ivy-covered trees, the path snaking round... of course, the painting. Only the bluebells were missing.

'Come on,' said Lucy.

I watched, puzzled, as Lucy set about helping some younger girls drag branches across the path in two places, making barriers. A few yards away, towards the edge of the games field, Lorna led a team gathering dead leaves, earth, twigs and moss into a great heap, making another obstacle.

'What are we building?' I asked.

'Fences,' said Susanna, bending to scrape together an armful of leaves. 'It's like a mini gymkhana. We make fences and then jump over them, with faults given to anyone who makes a mistake.' In a lower voice she added, 'Lorna's favourite game.'

I bet it is, I thought. But there was nothing better to do, and for a while it was even quite fun, gathering piles of last year's leaves and balancing branches on tree stumps across the path.

Lorna strutted around giving instructions, deciding the distance between the jumps. When all was ready, she put us in a line with me at the end. 'Right,' she said. 'I'll show you the course first and you can take turns to follow. Remember to jump the fences in exactly the right order or you're disqualified. Giddy-up!' Tapping her imaginary horse on the flank with a stick, she galloped off.

I watched carefully as she jumped over the first branch, then a heap of leaves, approached the third jump from behind, doubled back for the next two, and generally wove between the trees to create a complicated pattern. Landing back with our group, she blew strands of hair from her face. 'Clear round,' she announced. 'OK, Nina, now you.'

I could swear Nina didn't get the order right but Lorna awarded her a clear round. The younger girls followed, one narrowly missing a fault by kicking leaves off the top of one of the heaps, and another only just clearing the water jump (the 'water' area in front of the fence being marked out with sticks). Susanna, skipping round the course, was ticked off for poor style, while Lucy got four faults for dislodging more leaves off the biggest heap, now showing signs of wear.

'But Katie did it too,' she protested, 'and you didn't give her any faults.'

'You don't have to take part, Lucy, if you don't want to,' said Lorna. 'And I'd have thought you'd know better than to question the judge.'

As Lucy, reddening, turned away, Lorna looked at me. My turn.

That's when I saw him. As I ran up to the first jump, there he was, standing between some saplings a few yards away, just where the woodland met the games field. Beside him a dog snuffled among the leaves, but it wasn't Webster. It was one I hadn't seen before: a kind of spaniel, its coat white and rusty brown mixed, with long hair and floppy ears. Catching my gaze, the boy broke into that same, almost blinding smile, raised something he held in his hands and pointed it straight at me.

A bow and arrow.

In mid-air over the jump, I ducked, caught my foot on the branch and fell to the ground.

'Fault,' said Lorna.

'Not fair,' I panted, rubbing my knees. 'I thought he was going to shoot me. That boy's a menace.'

'What boy?' said Nina.

'You know, David. Mrs Lockwood's son.'

'*David?*' said Lorna. 'How on earth… where is he?'

'He shouldn't be running around here,' said Lucy. 'It's much too far from Grange.'

'There.' Rising, I nodded over to the group of saplings. 'Oh.'

The rain had stopped. Sunlight breaking through clouds sent warm streaks across the thin grey trunks under their canopy of leaves. Nobody there. Not even a fair-haired boy with skinny arms and legs in grey shirt and shorts that couldn't have provided much protection from the rain.

'There's no one,' said Lorna. 'Nice try, Eleanor.'

'But I *saw* him.' Walking over to the saplings, I peered across the games field towards the cedar. The sun shone straight into my eyes but I could just make out a small figure running across the grass, hair lifting like thistledown in the breeze, dog bounding beside him. 'There.' I pointed. 'With the dog, see? I didn't know the Lockwoods had a spaniel.'

'A spa… what are you talking about?' Lucy came over, looked, and sighed. 'Oh, Eleanor. That's not a spaniel, that's Webster. He's a *retriever*.' Shaking her head, she walked back to the group.

I blinked. In the distance, people dotted the grass. Webster galloped among them, chasing balls and prompting shrieks of delight. No sign of David. Or his dog.

'Seriously?' said Nina. 'Ellie doesn't know the difference between a spaniel and a retriever?'

'Not Ellie,' put in Lucy, 'Eleanor.'

'Ellie, Eleanor – who cares?' said Nina. 'It's only a nickname.'

Only a nickname. Only a collection of sounds echoing another voice in another time and another place… My fingers made fists and I plunged them into my pockets.

'First refusal,' Lorna called over to me. 'You're eight faults down.'

I looked at her. 'I'm *what*?'

'Oh, Lorna, that's a bit harsh,' said Susanna. 'She doesn't know the rules.'

'She has to learn,' said Lorna. 'We all had to. Eleanor, you're off the course. Knocked down the first fence and avoided the second.'

'I haven't avoided anything, I was just trying to see—'

'A spantriever,' murmured Nina, 'or a retraniel. You said.' Closing her lips in a half-smile, she raised one eyebrow.

The younger girls giggled. Lucy walked over to stand beside Lorna. 'Look, Eleanor,' she said, 'if you get faults you have to accept them. Making up stories won't help.'

Nina sniggered. 'I can't wait for her first riding lesson,' she said. 'Will she be able to tell the ponies apart, do you think? If she has such trouble with dogs…'

I never heard the rest. Through the roaring in my brain Susanna's voice came faintly, as if from far away – 'Nina, that's really mean' – but I could no longer see her face or anyone's face because of the way they all blurred into each other. I pushed my hands down into my pockets so hard they stretched the seams, but I knew I couldn't take them out because if I did… if I did…

Head down, I charged. Figures jumped out of my way; who they were, I couldn't tell. Reaching the biggest pile of leaves, I kicked and kicked, scattering leaves and twigs far and wide until nothing remained of the jump that had taken the longest to build. Yells and exclamations from behind echoed inside me, and for a second I longed to look round, to let the image of those faces, however angry and jeering, wipe out another far, far worse picture that had shot to the surface of my mind.

I didn't dare. Hurling myself down the path, out of the wood and across the games field, I fought with all my strength to push down the memory of my last day at West Hill, as raw and fresh and bloody now as it was then, all those weeks ago.

CHAPTER SEVEN

Laughter in the Dark

Nobody spoke to me at supper. News of what happened in the woodland had spread, and the people at my table edged away, half nervous, half fascinated, as if I were some wild creature that had to be watched. Lorna, Nina and Lucy sat as far away as they could, and Susanna – the only one who might have been kind – was stuck on a different table.

I concentrated on eating the slab of thick white bread and ham in my hand, but the chunks went round and round in my mouth, refusing to be swallowed. Why would no one believe me? Just because he scampered off before anyone came to look, the dog running behind him... Oh yes, the dog! As Mrs Lockwood came by, checking we were eating up properly, it was on the tip of my tongue to ask about the spaniel, just to prove to the others that I wasn't as stupid as they thought; but then it struck me that I might get David into trouble. Besides, Mrs Lockwood's straight back and deep-set eyes didn't make her easy to talk to.

Susanna waited for me in South Hall as we came out. 'Are you all right?' she said.

I nodded.

Taking my arm, she pulled me to one side, away from the people heading for the door to the garden. Late sunshine broke through the clouds, offering a last half-hour of play on the open grass before bedtime. We'd have to follow, but for the moment Susanna held me back.

'Really all right?' She studied my face.

Tears sprang to my eyes. Blinking, I nodded more fiercely than before. 'Thanks,' I managed to squeeze out.

'What for? They were horrible to you. I don't blame you for wrecking that jump.'

'You don't?'

'Not one bit. Lorna's always been bossy but she seems to have it in for you. Nina too. They still think it's your fault they're not in the same dorm.'

'I know. But it isn't!' My voice came out louder than I'd intended. 'I never even wanted to come here! I'd be back at home right now if it hadn't been for…' I stopped, biting my lip. 'I mean,' I mumbled, 'it's up to Mrs Fielding who she puts where.' Turning away, I let my hair fall across my face, hiding the blood rushing into my cheeks.

A pause. I could feel Susanna's eyes on me. *Don't ask*, I thought. *Just don't.*

''Course it is,' she said after a moment. 'They're just

44

being silly. They'll get over it.' She grabbed my arm. 'Come on, or the bell for bedtime will go before we've had a chance to play outside.'

I could have hugged her. Instead I let her pull me through the door, down the steps and onto the path skirting the house. Before us, a long, tightly clipped hedge of box trees blocked our view, raindrops on the tiny leaves sparkling in the low sun. Shading our eyes, we turned left towards the games field, where girls slithered across the wet grass playing tag, or scrambled up the branches of the cedar. Yet it was what lay on the other side of the cedar that drew my gaze: the chapel on its small mound, and beyond it, the roofline and walls of Grange, showing here and there between the trees.

'If you're looking for David,' said Susanna, 'he won't be out now. Mrs Lockwood will be putting him and Alice to bed.'

Of course. It was 6.30 pm after all. 'Do you think she knows what he gets up to when she's not around?' I said. 'Him and his dog?'

Susanna tucked a curl behind her ear. 'I don't think she can do,' she said, 'or she'd fetch him back. If he *is* running free, that is.'

'That's what I th—' I began, and stopped.

If.

Even Susanna didn't believe me.

In the dorm that night I focused on undoing my shoes, folding my clothes on my chair, rearranging all my things

– safer for Loki to nestle inside my bedside box than to risk being knocked off the top, I decided – anything so as not to look at Lorna and Lucy exchanging silent glances opposite. Even so, I could feel their pointed stares every time I turned my back.

'Coming to the bathroom?' said Susanna, already in her dressing gown.

What, and give those two the chance to talk about me the moment I was out of the room? 'You go,' I said. 'I won't be long.'

Susanna hesitated. Lucy came over and put her arm through hers. 'Probably best to leave Eleanor,' she said, 'if that's what she wants.'

'Yes,' said Lorna. 'We don't want to upset her, do we?'

Heat rose to my cheeks. Bending down, I lunged under the bed for my slippers. 'Please go,' I said as the floor blurred to a dark brown smudge before my eyes. '*All* of you.' I'd have held on to Susanna if I could, but not with Lorna and Lucy thrown in as well. Susanna must have sensed this because when I looked up again, the room was empty.

Taking a few deep breaths, I put on my slippers and tightened the bow on my dressing gown. If I timed it right, I'd reach the bathroom just as they were all finishing. If wrong, I'd be told off by Mrs Fielding, who, judging by her voice in the distance, was halfway to Fairfax on her evening rounds. Walking to the door, I opened it … and nearly tripped over the threshold.

The passage lay in darkness. Someone – I had a pretty good idea who – had turned off the light and closed the bathroom door. Hampden dorm, nearby, was no help; lights out for the younger girls had happened at least twenty minutes ago. Cursing Lorna under my breath, I scrabbled all around the door frame for the switch before giving up and feeling my way along the wall.

Only a few steps. Ten, fifteen at most. Gradually light filtered in from the half open door to Fairfax behind me, while thin white strips ahead outlined the entrance to the bathroom. Aiming for that, I forced my breathing to stay calm. *It's just a bit of darkness*, I told myself. *It's nothing. Any second now, someone will open the door and you'll be standing here, blinking like an idiot.*

My heart lurched. My hand, guiding me along the wall, fell into nothingness. A shadowy blackness, deeper and stronger than any yet, opened before me, like the mouth of a cave. A chill gust brushed my cheek, and I staggered back, knocking my shoulder on something hard and sharp. It took me a second to realise I'd fallen against the edge of the wall where the passage turned the corner, and that the cold draught must be coming from a door standing open somewhere along it. Yes – down there, in the direction of the laughter.

Laughter. I stood as still as stone. Ahead, no crack of light from Mrs Fielding's or Chloe's bedrooms relieved the gloom. All was silent. Yet that broken, exultant sound echoed in my ears and I stared into the darkness until my eyes ached, willing for some explanation – any, no matter how unlikely – of who could possibly be laughing down there.

A door opened behind me. I jerked round, shielding my eyes as light flooded the corridor.

'*There* you are,' said Susanna. 'I was getting worried. Hey, why's it dark round here?'

I didn't reply. I could only look at her, relief coursing through my limbs, my breath coming in gulps as if after some great exertion.

Lorna's arm appeared over Susanna's shoulder, reaching for the wall just by her ear. 'Who switched these off?' she said, as the overhead lamps blazed into life. 'Oh, Eleanor. Of course.'

'*Me?*' I gaped as she stalked past. 'Y-you did it! It must have been you.'

'Ssh,' said Lucy, nodding towards Hampden. 'You'll wake the little ones. And anyway, why would Lorna do that? You can't go around falsely accusing people, Eleanor.' Shaking her head, she followed in Lorna's wake.

'I—'

'Take no notice,' said Susanna, holding the bathroom door open. 'Just be quick before Mrs Fielding wonders where you are.'

No time for a shower. Washing as fast as I could, I turned the past five minutes over and over in my thoughts. What a dope to let my imagination run away with me, just because someone switched off the lights!

That had to be Lorna; who else? And the laughter… obviously that was her. She knew how scared I'd be. The darkness disorientated me, that was all, making it sound as if the noise was coming from down the corridor instead of the bathroom. Easy to lose all sense of direction in the dark.

Well, she wouldn't get me that way again. In future I'd take my torch.

CHAPTER EIGHT

Happiness is a Shetland Pony

'Told you you'd get Happy, Eleanor.'

Get – *happy?*

Standing by the noticeboard at break on Monday, Lucy called me over. 'Beginners' ride at two o'clock. See?' Flicking her hand at the board, she disappeared through the door to the boot room.

My stomach leapt. I was going to learn to ride *today*! I ran my gaze down the rounders team lists to the scrap of paper pinned below. Yes, there was my name, and next to it…

Ah. That was what Lucy meant. Reading which pony I'd been given, all I could see was the curve of a red-and-white neck fringed by a shaggy mane, and a pair of large, stony eyes fixed on my lower leg. How could anyone have named him Happy?

'Don't worry,' said Susanna, coming up beside me. 'Just remember to hold the reins really tight as you mount so he can't turn his head. I'd give you a hand but I'm on the three o'clock ride.' She nodded at another notice nearby.

'With Lorna and Lucy, I suppose?' I said.

'Oh no, they're not intermediates, they're advanced,' said Susanna. 'Nina too. You have to remember,' she added, as we headed indoors for our milk and biscuits, 'they've been riding all their lives. Not like you and me.'

You and me. It felt like a hug. My heart lifted as I followed Susanna into the dining hall. Everything would be OK. It might take a while for me to ride like Ricky in *Champion the Wonder Horse*, but I'd manage Happy, no problem.

So, after lunch, while the others lay on their beds reading books, I battled with my riding clothes. The boots were all right but the jodhpurs felt worn and too big around the waist, and I'd already noticed that everyone else's hat was black, not brown. As I placed mine on my head, I caught Lorna turning away to hide a smile.

Grabbing my gloves – faded, stained – I thrust them in my jacket pocket. I knew it had been a mistake buying second-hand clothes, I knew it! But then I saw Mum's face as we trawled the shops and the way her eyes lit up when she spotted these in the charity shop window, and for a moment I couldn't think about anything else. I left the dorm without looking right or left.

'Have fun!' Susanna called after me. I couldn't reply.

Down the stairs, across the dining hall, through to the boot room, and out into the playground. By the time my heels stopped clattering and sank instead into the soft earth and sawdust of the stable yard, I let my shoulders relax. It helped that none of the other girls making for the stables – younger ones, of course, this being the beginners' group – seemed bothered by my outfit. Once my eyes – and nose – adjusted to the inside of the building, I found Happy in his stall, where Carla, who worked in the stables, joined me.

'Right,' she said, heaving a saddle onto Happy's broad back. 'This is how you tack up. Take the girth' – she pointed to the strap hanging down Happy's far side – 'and buckle it so you can just fit two fingers between it and the pony. He'll puff out his tummy to stop you – there, he's doing it already – but you mustn't let him. Tighter, tighter…'

I struggled with the buckles.

'Not *too* tight. You don't want to hurt him, do you?'

No, I thought. *But he could make it easier, bother him.*

'Now the bridle.' Throwing the reins over Happy's head, Carla lifted the straps in place over his ears with one hand while, with the other, she held the bit against his lips. Two rows of strong yellow teeth remained firmly closed. 'C'mon, Happy,' she murmured.

I looked at Carla's bare hand pushing against Happy's resisting bite and made up my mind. This was something I was not going to do, ever.

'There.' As Happy – resentfully – took the bit, Carla gave his short red-and-white (oh, all right, *skewbald*, thank you, Lucy) neck a pat. 'Next time you can manage on your own. Now, lead him out – no, not like that.'

She rolled her eyes as I gave the bridle a yank. 'Stand by his head and walk, looking forwards. That's better.'

'Ha, Eleanor. I wondered who we were missing.' In a green padded jacket over shirtsleeves, jeans and wellington boots, Mrs Lockwood greeted me as I emerged, blinking, into the yard, trying not to drag Happy, who seemed to have trouble lifting his hooves. Around her, half a dozen small girls – squits, as Lorna called them – sat already on their ponies.

As Mrs Lockwood showed me how to mount, I remembered Susanna's advice and held the reins tightly. I could swear Happy's head twitched as I clambered into the saddle but, finding Mrs Lockwood standing between his teeth and my ankle, he thought better of it.

This time.

Sliding my legs over the long bench at supper that evening, I couldn't suppress a grimace.

Susanna, sitting opposite, gave a grin. 'Stiff, eh? How was the ride?'

I thought about Happy refusing to move, then walking round the riding school in a way that hurled me from side to side, as if the saddle were a small boat on a rolling sea. 'OK,' I said.

'Did Happy behave?'

'He wouldn't walk, wouldn't trot when we had to trot, and wouldn't stop trotting when it was time to walk again. Otherwise fine.'

'Sounds normal for Happy.'

Supper consisted of tinned spaghetti, but I was so hungry I didn't care. Digging in, I felt eyes watching me from further up the table and, looking round, saw Lorna and Lucy. No sign of Nina. She must be sitting elsewhere; no wonder Lucy looked so pleased. Catching my gaze, the two of them dropped theirs and whispered together, Lucy nodding solemnly.

I put my fork down. On my plate, spaghetti worms swam in congealing red sauce.

They were plotting something, I knew it.

At bedtime I entered the dorm with Susanna to find Lorna sitting on her bed with her arms crossed, while Lucy stood by the window.

'Eleanor,' said Lorna, 'I was really upset by what you did yesterday.'

'Yes,' said Lucy. 'You spoilt it for everybody.'

'But we've decided to give you a second chance,' said Lorna. 'Your first week at Ashstone is nearly up, which means it's time for your initiation task.'

'What initiation task?' I said.

'Every new girl has to do one,' said Lorna. 'Didn't Susanna tell you?'

'Oh, *that*,' said Susanna. 'It's just a bit of messing around. Like getting you to sneak into Verney and throw a pillow at someone.'

'I could do that,' I said.

Lorna shook her head. 'Too easy.'

'All right, then.' Susanna bounced onto her bed

and sat swinging her legs. 'We could get her to creep into the bathroom after lights out and mix up all the washbags and towels on hooks. There'll be chaos in the morning.'

Lorna and Lucy exchanged looks.

'Actually,' said Lorna, 'we've decided on something already. Late tonight. After all the matrons have stopped patrolling.'

'Why?' said Susanna. 'Dodging Stalkie is half the fun.'

'It has to be then, because what Eleanor's going to do is walk out of Fairfax, go round the corridor and come back in from the other side.'

'What?' Susanna stopped swinging her legs.

'I said,' repeated Lorna, 'she's got to walk round the corridor—'

'No. That's too much, Lorna. You can't make her do that.'

'Oh, can't I?' Lorna stood up. 'After what she did to us yesterday?'

I looked from one face to another, sickness rising inside me. Groping the short way to the bathroom the night before had been bad enough; but to go further, to turn towards that mouth of darkness and walk through it, cold air lifting the hair on the back of my neck, while at any moment a voice could crack the silence, a snatch of laughter, that might be my imagination playing tricks, but might not...

And then the Huntsman.

My legs seemed to go from under me. I sat down on my bed.

Through a buzzing in my ears came Susanna's voice, stronger than before. '*Even* after yesterday. It's just too far and too scary. Besides, if she gets caught, there'd be a real row, much more than if it was only a prank on another dorm. Let's think of something fun for her to do.'

Lorna shrugged. 'No one's making her do it. Up to her. If she hasn't got the guts...'

'But you're asking much more of her than anyone else,' Susanna protested. 'Suppose – suppose she meets the Huntsman?'

'Oh, *Susanna*,' said Lucy in her best grown-up voice, 'you don't *really* believe that nonsense, do you?'

I gaped at her. '*You* believe it,' I said. 'Or you did last week.'

She snorted. 'I didn't really.'

'Well, you could have fooled me.' I fixed her with my eyes. She smiled straight back.

Lorna stepped in. 'All we're asking you to do, Eleanor, is walk round the corridor,' she said. 'What's so bad about that? It's not like at my cousin's school. They once made a boy there strip naked and run round the playground.'

'What?' I said. 'Did no one stop him?'

'Dunno. It was ages ago. People had to do far worse things in the old days. Don't see why you're making such a fuss now about a short walk, just because it's after lights out.'

This was too much. Even from her. 'I'm not!' I cried. 'I haven't said I won't do it, have I?'

Lorna's eyes gleamed. 'So you will?'

I was in for it now. 'Yup,' I said, holding her gaze.

'And you're not scared of... *the Huntsman*?'

'Huh.' I made my voice sound as strong as I could. 'That's just a story someone's made up. To frighten people,' I added, looking hard at Lucy.

'Like the ones you make up, I suppose?' she flashed back. 'To explain why you're useless at jumping fences?'

'Shut up, Lucy,' said Lorna. Putting her head on one side, she nodded and said, 'Good for you.'

I felt warm inside, suddenly. I don't know why.

'Eleanor.' Susanna leaned forwards. 'You don't have to do this. Lorna, whatever you say about yesterday, this isn't fair. It's not what we usually do.'

'Yes, well, sometimes people have to make up for things,' said Lorna. 'If Eleanor wants to be one of us...'

That did it. 'It's OK, Susanna,' I said. 'I'll be fine. Don't worry.' Bending down, I began to undo my shoes so she couldn't catch my eye and make me waver. Not now I'd steeled myself to go through with it.

'Why are you girls not ready for bed?' Mrs Fielding entered, Beaky on her shoulder. Without thinking I looked up, only to see her eyes glance off mine as if they'd met an electric shock.

My hand stopped in the middle of pulling off my socks. Had the others noticed how the headmistress avoided me? It didn't look like it, from the way they hurried into their dressing gowns. Besides, Beaky chose that moment to stage a diversion by hopping from Mrs Fielding's shoulder to one of the chests of drawers, from there to the top of Lucy's bedside box and so on around the room, his beak jabbing at any hand that tried to brush him away. When at last Mrs Fielding coaxed him back to her shoulder and order was restored, I finished changing into my own dressing-gown, trying out various answers in my head in case questions did arise. *Just don't think about it*, I decided. *No one will find out what you did if you don't tell them.*

After all, I had something bigger to worry about right now. Forcing myself to saunter to the bathroom for a shower, I chatted to the others as if all was fine and dandy, as if the task ahead didn't bother me in the least; while inside something built up and built up till I shook so much I couldn't get my arms into my pyjama sleeves.

Later, watching Lorna thrust her clock under her blankets so that when midnight came the alarm wouldn't wake the whole school, I hoped with all my heart that the blasted thing would fail to go off.

CHAPTER NINE

The One-Legged Huntsman

Someone was shaking me. Angie's face floated next to mine, eyes squeezed shut so only the lashes showed, lips moving. She was begging me to do something, and I tried to answer but my mouth wouldn't open; I could say nothing while she held my shoulders and shook and shook...

I opened my eyes. This was Ashstone, not West Hill. Angie belonged to another life. And the person shaking me was Lorna. 'At last,' she muttered. 'You are a heavy sleeper, aren't you? The others are awake already.'

I sat up. From the bed next to me, a dark shape leaned across the gap. 'I'll come with you,' said Susanna. 'You're not going alone.'

Yes, oh yes! My chest rose. With Susanna for company...

'Where's the point in that?' whispered Lorna, back in the safety of her bed. 'We'll only have to think up another task. I'm not setting my alarm for midnight again.'

The wave inside me ebbed. Under my feet the floor felt cold and hard as I swung my legs down. Hunting for my slippers, I said to Susanna, 'I'll be back before you know it. May even bring a one-legged friend, if he looks a bit lonely.'

'Eek!' Stifling a giggle, Susanna dived under her pillow before raising her head again and whispering, 'Good luck!'

'Thanks.' Shuffling into my dressing gown, I felt deep into my bedside shelf for my torch, and my fingers closed on a round, comforting shape with straggly hair. Slipping Loki into one pocket and the torch into the other, I made my way to the door, the thought of the troll's cheerful expression giving a lightness to my step. It would all be OK. I could do this.

I tiptoed into the corridor and a floorboard gave a thunder crack. Heart thumping, I waited for Mrs Fielding to come storming round the corner. But except for the sound of regular breathing and the odd cough from Hampden's open door – warm, human noises that made me long to slip in there and curl up – all remained silent.

I crept on to where ghostly white shapes glimmering through the doorway showed me I'd reached the bathroom. This was the moment. Fighting the urge to whirl round and run back to the dorm, I forced myself to turn right, facing the passage that stretched away into darkness, ears pricked for a sound that could shatter the stillness at any moment.

None came.

Letting out my breath, I gripped the torch in my pocket. Its solid shape felt reassuring, but I didn't dare switch it on, not yet. First I had to get past Mrs Fielding's and Chloe's bedrooms, and then… and then… The image of a tall figure in black cloak and riding breeches rose before me, face invisible under the shadow of his hood, or else he had no face at all…

I stuffed my fist in my mouth, biting my knuckles hard. *Come on, Eleanor.* There was nothing – nobody – there.

Feeling for Loki in my left-hand pocket, I held him tight before stepping into the darkness. From Mrs Fielding's room came the sound of steady, even breathing, quietening my own. Did Beaky sleep there too, I wondered, perched on the end of her bed, head tucked under a shiny black wing?

The picture made me smile. This wasn't so bad. A few more steps and I could switch on the torch and the worst would be over.

As I passed Chloe's room, my stomach turned over. From inside the door came a rattle and a scraping of metal, followed by an arrow of light darting into the corridor.

No time to think. I threw myself beyond the reach of the light, my shoulder hitting a recess on the other side of the passage, my fingers brushing a door handle. In an instant I turned the handle, slipped through the door and closed it behind me. Leaning my whole back against the door, breathing so hard I could see my chest rising and falling, I strained my ears for the sound of footsteps outside, praying that wherever Chloe was heading, it wasn't here.

After a moment I relaxed my shoulders, looked around – and my heart jumped right back into my throat.

There could be no mistaking where I was. Five feet away, a criss-cross-patterned window – twin of the one in Fairfax – let in a dim light. Dust covered the sill and the basin below it, while on the left I could just make out the shape of a lavatory, its pipe leading to an ancient cistern high above. To the right…

My head wouldn't move. I couldn't look. Not to see a tall figure in riding cape and hunting leather separate itself from the wall and lunge towards me…

I thought my chest would explode. Thrusting my hand into my pocket, I switched on the torch so that, as soon as I drew it out, trembling, light danced up and down the walls. Shadows glided into each other, revealing the shapes of an old wicker basket, a fishing rod, two tennis rackets, their strings unravelling, and in the corner to my right… I stifled a scream.

A bright, black eye stared back at me.

The next moment the scream evaporated as the beam outlined a dappled horse's head mounted on a long red-brown stick, the paint faded and chipped, one end of some leather reins fixed in place, the other broken off and trailing on the floor. A child's toy, old and much loved. If *that* was the Huntsman's steed, I didn't have much to fear from him.

I stood for a few seconds, waiting for my breathing to die down. So this was the famous haunted loo! Nothing but a storeroom now. Dust and flakes of paint covered the surfaces, while cobwebs masked the shelf above the cistern and the shapes lying there: a hatbox, a couple of suitcases, a man's leg…

I all but dropped the torch. Clasping one hand over my mouth, I fought with the other to hold the beam steady, sending shadows rocketing up the wall before picking out once more the long, dark boot, lying flat so that the foot pointed up at the end.

The long, dark boot. A leather riding boot poking out of the gloom; presumably its fellow lay stuck behind the big old-fashioned suitcase beside it.

I let my head fall back against the door, lips pressed together to keep back the laughter. Had I just stumbled upon the source of the Legend of the One-Legged Huntsman? It looked like it. If so… and now an idea blazed into my mind, causing me to hug myself tight to prevent the laughter bursting out. Lucy thought it was all nonsense, did she? We'd see about that.

Dropping my arms, I stood up straight. Time to move on. The others would be wondering where I'd got to; and while I couldn't care less if my absence began, just a little, to worry Lorna and Lucy, Susanna was a different matter. Switching off the torch, I opened the door and peeped out.

A diamond of light from Chloe's room fell across the corridor. What could she be doing, wandering around the house at night, not even bothering to shut the door behind her? Perhaps she used the light for guidance, not wanting to disturb others by switching on the one in the passage. It certainly made my task easier. Except for the risk of running into her, of course.

I should have turned right and carried on down the corridor, but the glow just a few steps away drew my eyes and before I knew it, I stood on the threshold of Chloe's room, taking in every detail. The first thing that struck me was that Chloe hadn't just left her bed; she'd not been in it. The velvety coverlet on the great oak four-poster lay in place. No clothes were draped over the shabby armchair in the corner of the room. Over the fireplace on the left hung a painting of a man in uniform; a full-length portrait, it looked like, though in the poor light cast by the bedside lamp I could make out no more than the peak of his cap and a hint of medals across his chest. I didn't dare look closer. Any minute now Chloe could come down the corridor, and while she normally drifted around the school seeing nobody, even she could hardly fail to notice an eleven-year-old girl in a dressing gown standing in her bedroom doorway.

Turning away, I stared into the darkness, willing my eyes to adjust from the light now lying behind me. Too risky to switch on the torch, with Chloe at large. Taking a deep breath, I felt my way down, and before long the darkness faded into the open landing of the south stairs before thickening again towards the end of the passage, where the door frame of Cromwell – more squits, according to Lorna – stood out against the gloom. Another corner, another length of corridor, then the balcony over the hall, and I'd be home and dry.

Hand on the balustrade at the top of the stairs, I stopped. A few feet below, at the turn of the staircase, the top part of her body twisted round so that her arms rested on the windowsill, sat Chloe. Moonlight shone in, catching her hair and turning it silver. I was about to tiptoe on, thankful not to have been spotted, when something about the set of Chloe's head held me back. Beautiful though the moon was, her gaze was fixed elsewhere.

Very softly, I crouched down to bring myself close to her line of vision. Below the window lay the box garden, and beyond that, the woodland where – I recognised with a jolt – I'd disgraced myself the day before. The treetops stood out black against the sky, a single one highest and blackest of all. Seeing it wave in the night breeze, I could almost hear the branches creaking and the patter of rain on the leaves as we'd sheltered beneath it. Perhaps, having painted it on a summer's day, Chloe was studying how to do so by moonlight.

I crept on, past the sounds of breathing and snuffling from Cromwell's open door, round the corner and back into darkness. Now, surely, I could use the torch. Pointing the beam downwards to keep it low, I hurried past Stalkie's bedroom, her surgery next to it and the stairs to the top floor, and turned right along the balcony. No need for the torch here: the moon shone through the misted glass roof, its soft light picking out pieces of cutlery on the tables laid for breakfast. Then – oh, joy – the east stairs lay before me, Verney and Pym dorms opening out on my left, and, to the right, Fairfax. Running in, I threw myself onto my bed, the darkness breaking into shapes as three figures leapt off the bed next to mine.

'Eleanor – thank goodness!'

'Where have you been?'

'Did you get caught?'

It took so long to catch my breath that for a moment all I could do was shake my head. 'No,' I managed at last, 'I didn't get caught.'

'But what happened?' whispered Lucy. Back under her own blankets, she picked up her watch from beside her bed. 'You've been gone twenty-five minutes!'

'Susanna was all for going after you,' said Lorna from her corner. 'But we wouldn't let her. We wanted to give you a chance.' Dark as it was, I could see the tilt of her chin, as if challenging me to disagree.

'Thanks,' I said. Leaning right out of my bed, I reached my arm across to Susanna in hers, but the gap was too great. 'I'm fine,' I whispered. 'Don't worry.'

'Phew,' she whispered back.

'So what happened?' repeated Lucy. 'Oh, I suppose you met the… *Huntsman*?' The faintest pause before the word.

I grinned into the darkness. 'Well…'

Lucy gasped. 'You did?'

'I – I can't talk about it,' I said. 'Not now. Please – leave me alone.' Burrowing under my pillow, I stifled the laughter erupting inside me. If Lorna and Lucy thought my trembling came from fear, so much the better.

I don't know how long I lay there – probably just a few minutes, but it felt much longer – letting the pillow muffle the urgent whispering from the beds opposite, begging me to talk. Finally they gave up, and I drifted off to sleep.

The next morning, Lucy tucked her arm into mine and escorted me down to breakfast. 'I want to hear all about it,' she said.

'Me too,' said Lorna on the other side. 'Tell us, Eleanor.'

I could get used to this, I thought. Never in my life had I been this popular. 'I – I can't. Not yet.' Disengaging my arm from Lucy's, I turned round for Susanna. 'Tonight, perhaps. If I can, that is.' I let a shudder run down my back.

'Can what?' Nina drew alongside.

Lorna waved her away. 'Tell you later.'

Nina's mouth fell open, sending a wave of inexpressible delight through me. Dangerous, but, oh, for now it felt so good. Even if there'd be a price to pay, it was worth it to see Nina's habitual one-eyebrow-raised smile wiped, however briefly, from her face.

I kept Lorna chatting, Lucy hanging on behind. Sitting down for breakfast, I turned to Susanna and managed, unseen by the others, to give her a wink. Fun as it was to keep Lorna and Lucy on tenterhooks, Susanna deserved better, and if I could have grabbed a moment before the evening to confide in her I would have done. But opportunities for private conversations were rare at Ashstone.

That night, by the time we were tucked up in bed, I was ready. Keeping an eye out for the approach of Sulky Sal, the duty matron, I began by describing the creaking floorboards, the ghostly light from the bathroom and the thick, suffocating darkness of the forbidden corridor. 'Then,' I let my voice drop, 'as I passed the haunted loo, an icy draught lifted the hair from the back of my neck.'

From the beds around me came sharp intakes of breath.

'So I looked round. I could have sworn the door was shut, but there it stood, half open.'

A gasp from Susanna. 'What did you do?'

'I carried on, fast as I could, and didn't look back. And…' I paused. 'That's when it began.'

'What did?' asked Lorna.

'A noise. Quiet, at first. So quiet, I barely heard it. But then it grew louder.'

'Wh-what sort of noise?' whispered Lucy.

'A kind of thump… dr-a-a-a-g. Thump… dr-a-a-a-g. Like someone limping. Limping really badly.'

Lucy gave a little scream. 'No! The Huntsman!'

'At the end of the corridor I couldn't help it; I *had* to look round.'

'What did you see?' A squeak of bedsprings as Susanna bounced into a sitting position.

'Nobody, of course,' said Lorna.

'I thought that at first.' I paused for as long as I dared. 'But then the moon shone through the window on the landing and I could see something moving between the banisters and the wall.'

'Stop,' said Lucy. 'You're scaring me.' Her head, silhouetted against the panelling, disappeared from view as she slid under her bedclothes.

Taking care to make no sound, I leaned over the side of my bed and picked up my shoe.

'No, go on,' said Lorna. 'This is good.'

'I ran like the wind, round the corner and along the next passage. But the sound just kept coming closer and closer. Thump… dr-a-a-a-g. Thump… dr-a-a-a-g, thump… dr-a-g, thump drag, thump*drag*, *thumpdrag*, until it was right behind me and…'

Raising my arm, I hurled my shoe as hard as I could at Lucy's bed. It didn't matter that it fell near the edge before clattering harmlessly to the floor. Lucy's scream must have woken the whole school, or at least all the dorms surrounding Fairfax.

We were in such trouble. The next morning we had to get up early and lie spreadeagled on the balcony floor (a favourite Ashstone punishment) while Mrs Fielding lectured us on Talking After Lights Out. Not only that: for the rest of the week we lost half an hour of reading time, having our lights switched off at the same time as Hampden, much to the amusement of the younger girls. I was afraid the others would blame me, and Lucy did, before accepting that I'd never have thought up the story had she and Lorna not set me such a scary task in the first place.

'Well done,' said Susanna in my ear as we crossed the playground towards the classroom block after assembly. 'That was really brave of you. And funny.'

I grinned. Maybe I could handle this place after all. Lorna might still not be my friend, but there was something measured in the way she looked at me now; as if I were worth considering. Everything would be OK from now on.

CHAPTER TEN

Playing Games

At break on Thursday morning, I scanned the table where our letters were laid out and felt a little leap inside at the sight of Mum's black ink and spidery writing. Tearing open the envelope, I settled down to read. Halfway down the page I stopped as the words jumbled and ran together so much I couldn't make them out.

It didn't matter. I knew what Mum was saying. Dad too. He'd written, 'So sorry, darling' above his signature at the bottom of the page, with lots of kisses, but I knew he wasn't, not really. He'd been desperate to go to America, and here at last, with this three-week lecture tour arranged by the wretched Society of Historical Architects, or Architectural Historians, or something, he had his chance. And it was important for his career, I knew that. But why couldn't it have happened in the summer holidays? We could all have gone then! No, it had to be now, which meant he wouldn't be able to drive down this Sunday with Mum and take me out. Or next Sunday. Or the one after that. My throat felt thick, and more tears prickled my eyes.

'What's the matter?' Susanna appeared in front of me, sucking the straw of her milk bottle.

I shook my head, unable to speak.

Lucy picked up my untouched bottle. It was what we got for break, with a couple of dull biscuits. 'Better drink this,' she said. 'Mrs Lockwood's watching.'

Bossy as ever, but her tone held a note of sympathy, giving me a twinge of guilt for the fright I'd given her. Taking the bottle from her outstretched hand, I nodded my thanks and let the liquid soothe my throat. Then I told them about Mum's letter.

'Oh, that's too bad about your dad,' said Lucy. 'But at least you'll see your mum.'

'She can't drive,' I said. 'And it takes too long to get here by train.'

It took Lucy and Susanna a moment to take this in.

'So you won't see them *at all*?' said Lucy. 'Not till half-term?'

'That's tough when you're new,' said Susanna. 'At least I'm used to it.'

'What?' For a second I forgot my own disappointment. 'Don't your parents ever come down?'

She shrugged. 'Hardly ever. It's too far from London. And Dad works most weekends. It's the same for lots of people,' she added, jerking her head round the dining hall, where other girls stood in groups, sucking straws and reading letters.

Hope soared in my chest. 'We can stick together,' I said.

'No… er, sorry.' Susanna looked at Lucy. 'Lucy's taking me out. I – we didn't know you'd be here on your own. Without any of us, I mean.'

'I'm only allowed one friend,' said Lucy.

Of course. Why shouldn't Susanna go out with Lucy? And why ever should Lucy include me, even if she were allowed, when we hadn't exactly hit it off? The look in Lucy's eyes confirmed my thoughts, try as she might to disguise it.

'It's only Sunday afternoon,' said Susanna. 'It'll fly past, like last—' She stopped, avoiding my eye.

Not difficult. I too had no wish to remember the Sunday before. I sucked up the last of my milk as noisily as possible and walked over to put the empty bottle in the crate by the door to the passage. 'Time to go,' I said. 'Don't want to be late for maths.'

Crossing the playground, I chattered away to Susanna and Lucy, showing how little I cared. It was only three weeks to half-term, after all. Really, not a long wait. I'd be fine.

I kept this up for most of the day, but when the time came to change for games, I cracked. Running to the bathroom, I splashed my face with hot water till my skin felt warm and puffy all over, not just round the eyes, and it just looked as if I'd had a really good wash. Not been crying my eyes out.

By the time I entered the boot room, everyone else was already on their way to the rounders pitch. Putting on my games shoes, I trailed after them, dragging my feet, kicking showers of gravel into the air.

'Wait for me!'

I looked up. From the direction of Grange, David came galloping over the grass towards me, a hobby horse between his legs.

'Race you there!' he cried, pulling the horse's head up and down as if trying to hold him back.

For a split second I was back in the haunted loo, a bright eye staring at me from out of the darkness... until I gave myself a shake. David's toy was nothing like the old one in the Huntsman's loo. It looked brand new, with bright red handles, smart leather reins and a flowing black mane. Funny how you can wait years for a hobby horse and then two come along at once.

'Ready, steady—'

'What?' My eyes snapped back to the rider bobbing before me. 'Race you where?'

He stopped still. Looked at me. 'To the lime tree, of course. Where else?'

I followed his gaze towards the woodland. The lime tree: he must mean the huge one standing by itself, whose thick leaves gave such shelter from the rain. But to race there? Right now? It would mean charging through at least two separate games of rounders, as if the sight of Mrs Lockwood's little boy running free with the weird new girl would attract no notice at all.

Impossible. But for a wild moment the thought of dodging the game, with its rules of Hitting and Not Hitting, Running and Not Running, and escaping instead into the woodland, felt tempting.

I shook my head. 'I can't, David. I have to play games.'

He gave a shout of laughter. 'Yes, games! Like we used to play.' Letting go of the horse's handles, he shook his hands repeatedly, as if he'd just washed them and was in too much of a hurry to bother with a towel, while doubling up in delight.

I didn't know what to make of him. Right now, all I wanted to do was get away before someone saw me being claimed best friend by this gawky, excitable, odd little boy. Looking round, I braced myself for the sniggering; but the couple of girls hurrying past – late, like me – didn't give either of us a glance.

'I don't know what you mean,' I said. 'And I have to go now. Sorry.'

Twenty yards away, Mrs Harris, the games teacher, fixed her eyes on me. *Stop dawdling*, they said.

It was as if the strings holding a puppet slackened suddenly. His hands dropped back to rest on the hobby horse handles. His head drooped. 'You're always going away,' he said.

Something inside me melted. 'Look, I'm not going home this Sunday,' I said. 'I can play with you then. All right?' I might as well, I thought. I hadn't anyone else to hang around with.

He didn't reply at once. Just looked at me, a small line appearing between his eyebrows. 'But you *are* home,' he said. 'This is home.'

Lucy was right. He couldn't be more than six years old, this boy. Which would explain the hobby horse – a toy too childish for a nine-year-old, surely.

'It is home for you,' I said gently.

'Eleanor Cooke!' Someone had clearly reminded Mrs Harris of my name, and her voice boomed across the games field.

'I must go,' I said. 'I'll see you on Sunday.'

'Promise?'

'Yes.' I nodded. 'But please – no bow and arrow this time. You gave me such a fright.'

Up and down his head danced as his smile turned to laughter. 'I did, oh, I did!'

The rounders game had stopped. Faces turned in my direction as Mrs Harris stood, hands on hips, glaring at me. With a crow of delight, David geed up his hobby horse and made off in the opposite direction from the woodland, heading for the chapel.

Good, I thought. *He's taking a shortcut home to Grange.*

Relieved, I set off towards Mrs Harris, and only just missed colliding with a figure in a navy-blue dress striding towards me down the path skirting the house.

'Sorry, Chloe,' I stammered.

I suppose if I *had* crashed into her, upsetting all the brushes and paints that poked out of the canvass bag she carried, she'd have noticed. But as it was, not a glimmer went through those blue-grey eyes; I might just as well have not been there at all. Hurrying on, I couldn't help glancing back – Chloe, vague, drifting Chloe; what could she be planning to paint so urgently? – only to see her standing where I'd left her, looking around. After a moment she turned and retraced her steps along the side of the house in the direction of the woodland, walking at her normal, steady pace, as if that was where she'd been heading all along. Strange.

Reaching Mrs Harris, I panted my apologies and sped to a fielding position, praying that no balls would come my way. Not while I wrestled with so many puzzles, one towering over all the rest: who was this person David Lockwood mistook me for?

On the way back to the boot room after games, Lucy nudged me in the ribs. 'That was hilarious, just now, you running smack into Chloe.'

'Oh, you saw.'

'Certainly did.' She grinned. 'It's funny. I've never seen Chloe in a hurry before.'

'That's what I thought.' But my mind was only half on what she was saying. How long had Lucy been watching? Long enough to see David waylay me before heading back to Grange, or only from the moment Chloe arrived? I was about to ask her, when the memory of the previous Sunday – David appearing from nowhere, unseen by everyone except me – flooded back. I wasn't going through all that again.

Yet one thing she could help me with. 'Do you know what's the matter with Chloe?' I asked. 'Why she behaves so oddly – not seeing or talking to anyone, I mean?'

Lucy's face took on a solemn expression. 'Something sad happened to her a long time ago,' she said. 'Nobody quite knows what. Somebody – a boyfriend or fiancé, maybe – died, or abandoned her, or something, and—'

'Who's this, Chloe?' Susanna caught up with us as we crossed the drive.

'—she's never been the same since,' finished Lucy.

'Poor Chloe,' said Susanna. 'She just wanders the grounds, painting the flowers and trees, and pining for him.'

Or gazes out at them by moonlight, I thought. How sad to remain lonely and grieving for so long – years, probably – unable to let go of this man, whatever had happened to him. Then a thought struck me. 'Was he a soldier?' I asked.

'I don't know,' said Lucy. 'Could've been, I suppose, and got killed in the war. But I don't think the dates match. Chloe's not that old.'

'Isn't she?' She looked old enough to me.

Susanna's eyes glowed. 'Perhaps they were childhood sweethearts,' she said. 'But he ran away to war, because – because he wanted to prove how brave he was, and—'

'Oh, Susanna,' sighed Lucy.

My lips relaxed into a smile, but my thoughts flew to a portrait on the wall of a dimly lit bedroom. The figure in uniform: could he have been a boy not yet out of his teens? Impossible to tell in the gloom.

Reaching the boot room, we slipped off our games shoes and joined the rush upstairs to wash and change before tea. In all the chatter around me I heard nothing. All I could think of was Chloe, sitting at her dressing table every night, brushing her long hair, while the one man in all the world she longed to see again, and never would, looked down at her.

Compared to that, three weeks to half-term didn't seem so long after all.

CHAPTER ELEVEN

The Secret Place

Even so, it was hard to make my way to South Hall on Sunday for letter-writing, through a knot of girls waiting excitedly by the front entrance. Large drops of rain had begun to fall during chapel, and now, from the grey light and the hammering on the roof, the weather looked set for the day.

'Have fun,' I said to Susanna and Lucy as I passed.

'You too.' Lucy gave me a bright smile.

Susanna squeezed my hand.

As I passed Lorna and Nina, the door to the long porch opened, sending damp air gusting into the hall, and a short lady in a tweed skirt, green waxed jacket and headscarf patterned with horseshoes walked in. 'Good morning, Mrs Fielding,' she said, tidying away a lock of grey hair clinging to her cheek.

'Hello, Mrs Stevenson,' said Mrs Fielding. 'The girls are ready.'

Lorna, who'd been chatting and tossing back her hair, stopped mid-speech. Her eyes seemed to droop at the corners.

'Lorna. And Nina.' The lady looked them over, as if checking for anything that might be missing. 'Got your anoraks? Very wet out there.'

'Hello, Gran.' Lorna's voice had an odd note, almost a wobble. 'I thought Mummy was picking us up.'

'Not possible, I'm afraid. She's at a meeting about the summer fete. You should see her at tea.'

'And Daddy?'

'Sorting out flooding down at Long Field. A culvert's got blocked. Come along now, I've got Algy in the car and I don't want lunch to burn.' With a brief nod to Mrs Fielding, she headed back down the porch.

Stuffing their arms into anorak sleeves, Lorna and Nina hurried after her. 'So… we're having lunch with you?' said Lorna. Then, 'No, no, I didn't mean – of course, thank you, Gran…'

Exclamations and greetings drowned out the rest as other parents arrived, scattering raindrops in all directions. Threading my way through, I reached the door to the passage and turned left towards South Hall, while before me I still seemed to see Lorna and Nina, heads bowed, trailing after Lorna's grandmother.

Going out for the day didn't look so much fun if your parents were too busy to take you home.

I wrote to Mum – no point writing to Dad – and said I was all right and didn't mind not seeing them, but I did miss her and Dad very much. Even Robbie. I drew a picture of my first riding lesson, making Happy very fat with big teeth, and me looking nervous. Finishing quickly gave me time to write to Angie, and I told her that everything was fine, and drew Happy for her too, before going on to describe the dark corridors and the weird punishments and Beaky trying to peck us all the time. With luck she'd laugh and write back.

After lunch – cold and dismal; meat and salad with no dressing – came the happiest news of the day. Since the rain showed no sign of ceasing, we'd have to spend the afternoon indoors, playing board games, drawing, practising the piano (hmm… well, maybe) or – best of all – reading in the library. For the first time since arriving at Ashstone, I could curl up with a book, snug and dry, while the rain drummed on the windows, instead of being turfed outdoors to wander the grounds.

The library lay in the south-east corner of the house, across the corridor from the music room. The moment I entered, a wonderful smell filled my nostrils: a mixture of soft, worked leather, old paper, furniture polish and a sprinkling of dust. Closing my eyes, I breathed in and out a few times before looking around the room.

Shelves lined the walls from floor to ceiling. A few girls already sat draped over armchairs, paperbacks on their knees. Straight ahead, a tall sash window looked out onto the box garden, while to the left, a faded blue window seat hugging the bay just asked to be sat on. All I needed was a book, and here, in rows of red and gold, stood hundreds.

It took me a minute or two to realise that these books weren't for reading. Not unless you understood French or Latin, or an old English full of strange letters and spellings. I should have followed the other girls' example and fetched my own paperback from by my bed, but I didn't want to give up so easily. There must be *something* here I could read.

At last I saw it. In a shelf near the bay, a collection of small books with strong blue lettering on their spines. Much too young for me. Yet coming across the *Flower Fairies* series here, among all the unreadable books, felt like greeting old friends. Picking one at random, I sat down on the window seat and opened it. 'To Sparrow, Happy Christmas 1945' was written on the first page. No signature followed; only a pen-and-ink drawing of a small, round bird, presumably to go with the dedication.

My lips twitched. A family nickname, obviously. But who for? The book probably belonged to Chloe, given her love of flowers. Did Mrs Fielding see her as a sparrow? Why – because she hopped around as a little girl? It was hard to imagine her ever being little, let alone hopping around like a sparrow, especially one as fat as this. A giggle rose in my throat, only to be cut short as something outside the window caught my eye.

There, in the pouring rain, stood David. If you could call it standing, with his head nodding like mad, his eyes screwed into slits, and hands clutched to his sides, shaking. Seeing his bare limbs, shining wet, sticking out from the familiar short-sleeved shirt and shorts made me clench my own teeth against the cold. Our last meeting rushed into my mind, together with a pang of guilt. I never thought he'd hold me to my promise in this weather. Yet here he was, gesticulating and mouthing at me, as if the rain falling around him and spattering muddy droplets over his shoes and socks was nothing to worry about.

Pressing my lips together, I shook my head, trying to show with my eyes how sorry I was. But his nodding just became even more urgent and, bending forward, he made his hands into fists, knuckles red with cold.

I looked round. Any moment one of the girls sitting in chairs or on cushions on the library floor might glance up, catch sight of David and set off to find a teacher. He'd get a serious telling-off, and it would be all my fault because if I hadn't made that stupid promise, he'd be safe and warm in Grange right now, not dancing with rage in the rain!

Slipping out of the library, I tiptoed down the passage and into South Hall. In seconds, I was through the door and running left down the path leading around the corner to where David stood, a few yards from the library window. He was soaked. Water plastered his hair to the back of his neck and rivulets ran down his clothes, but I could see it wasn't just the rain making his face wet. He fixed me with red-rimmed eyes surrounded by lashes that stuck together, and blurted out, 'You p-promised! You promised!'

'David, it's raining. We can't play in the rain. I'm not allowed out and I'm sure you aren't either. Let's make it another day, OK?'

I don't think he heard a word. 'You *promised*,' he kept saying. 'Why didn't you come?' Fists clenched, he raised and lowered his eyebrows and chin repeatedly in a frown full of pain and anger, eyes never leaving my face.

Fear darted through me. What was the matter with this boy? I put out a shaky hand. 'Let's go in,' I said. 'I – I'll take you home.' There'd be no end of fuss but what could I do?

'No!' he shouted. 'Not till you come with me. I've got something to show you.' Turning towards the games field, he glared at me over his shoulder, eyebrows still working furiously.

'David—'

'Why do you keep calling me David? I'm Davey, don't you remember? Or even—'

'All right, Davey.' Going after him, I tried to grab his hand but he stuck it behind his back.

'You promised! Come on!'

I looked about me. There was no one, yet I had the oddest feeling we were being watched. I scanned the windows behind me; a mistake, since from this distance the glass looked blank, and when I turned back it was to see Davey already halfway across the games field. I had no coat, no hat; my shoes were the soft, indoor type, already losing their shape in the wet. Rain penetrated my jumper and stuck my shirt to my skin, and I shivered. But there ahead of me ran a six-year-old boy wearing hardly anything at all.

'Wait,' I called out. 'You'll catch cold – *wait*!'

I caught up with him at the far side of the field, in the corner between the hedge and the woodland. His eyebrows had settled and he was smiling, laughing even, flicking his hands in front of him, still completely unaware of the rain.

'Look!' he said.

I looked. The grass here grew thick and long, beyond the reach of the lawnmower.

'See?' he said. 'They're beginning to come out.'

'W-what are?' Shivering, I jumped from foot to foot. 'David – D-Davey – I'm f-freezing and so are you. *Please* will you—'

'*Look.*' Crouching, he pointed.

Now I saw. An inch away from Davey's finger, a thin stem reached out of the grass, curving over into a bell-like flower whose petals were patterned like tiny red-and-white chessboards. Dotted around it were dozens more, many closed in a long, pointed diamond shape, down which the rain dripped, gathering into a droplet of pure crystal.

He straightened up. 'The fritillaries,' he said. 'Aren't they beautiful?'

'Fritty-*whats*?' How did a six-year-old *know* such words?

He doubled up, clasping his hands together, as if this was the funniest thing he'd ever heard. 'Fritillaries!' he repeated. '*You* know that.'

'I—' I stopped.

Davey looked into my eyes, hugely enjoying the joke of my pretended ignorance.

I smiled. 'Of course,' I said. 'They're lovely.'

He nodded, exultant, his grin so broad his face hardly seemed able to contain it. 'I knew it,' he said. 'I knew they'd bring you out here.' Jumping up and down, he flicked his hands again; then, without warning, he turned and shot off into the woodland.

'Davey!' What *now*? 'Wait!'

He shouted something, inaudible through the pattering of raindrops on leaves.

Cursing him, myself, the rain, everything, I raced after him, slipping and slithering down the path, dodging the remains of Lorna's jumps, until a call from above brought me up short.

No. Please, no.

Beyond the path, the lime tree rose high into the dark grey sky. And there, astride a branch, about six feet from the ground, sat Davey.

My chest seized up. I started breathing high and fast, a cry forming somewhere at the back of my throat. *Don't startle him*, I told myself. *Keep calm.*

I took a few deliberate steps. 'Davey, I don't think we're supposed to climb that tree, especially in the rain. Come down.'

He shook his head. 'Not till you come up.'

'No, that's silly. Be a good boy, now, please.' Was that how you talked to a six-year-old? I couldn't remember.

'All right, I'll just go higher, then.' Pressing his hands down on the branch, he shuffled towards the trunk.

Above him the tree soared thirty, forty, fifty feet… My stomach tightened. I looked all round while the voice inside me rose to a screech. *Idiot, why did you go after him? If he falls it will be all your fault.* The woodland and the games field lay empty. If I ran back to the house for help, by the time I returned it might be too late.

'Don't move,' I said. 'I'll come, but—'

A whoop broke from behind a screen of leaves and shoots, somewhere near the centre of the tree.

'—you must stay where you are.'

'Yes, yes, come on!' The leaves rustled.

'*Promise!* Or… or' – I had an inspiration – 'I won't play with you again.'

The leaves stood still. Two hands, peeping through to clutch at shoots, trembled. 'Don't say that, Robin,' he whispered. 'Please don't say that.'

I could have bitten off my tongue. 'Davey, I'm sorry. I didn't mean that. Of course I'll play with you again.' The words poured out, I hardly knew what I was saying, while a single thought darted through me. *Robin. That's who he thinks I am.* Now I could sort it all out – once I'd got him down – and persuade him that whoever this Robin person was, it wasn't me.

Rubbing my hands together, I climbed the first branch, my spirits rising at its bone-dry touch. This wouldn't be too difficult. But by the third branch the bark became damper, and reaching up for the fourth, my feet slid as they sought solid holds. I clutched the branch to my chest, feeling it hard against my ribcage. 'Davey,' I panted, 'this is high enough. Let's go down.'

'Why? We've only just got here.'

I nearly lost my balance. The reply had come from nowhere, directly into my ear. I turned to see that the tree had divided into three or four separate trunks, with a mass of leafy shoots – like the ones at the base of the tree – filling spaces between. Following the direction of the voice, I brushed aside a cluster of leaves to reveal a V-shaped gap, through which Davey peeped, an irresistible eagerness in his eyes.

'Come on!' His face disappeared.

Setting my teeth, I pulled myself in after him, squeezing through the gap – and caught my breath.

It was as if we'd reached a clearing in a forest. Inside the thicket of shoots and trunks, the tangle of growth formed a kind of floor covered in the soft mulch of last year's leaves. Treading carefully, you could sit with your back against solid wood and chat to someone sitting opposite – as Davey was – completely invisible from the ground. A glorious, secret, undiscovered hide, silent save for the rain pattering on the canopy high above and the wind rustling in the leaves.

Neither of us spoke. Gazing around, I took in every detail. A dozen questions on the tip of my tongue clamoured for release, the loudest being: *How did a six-year-old find such a place, let alone reach it?* He'd scrambled up here as if he did it every day of his life; if so, his parents must know and not worry. Yet if Ashstone pupils were forbidden to climb this tree – and I was pretty sure we were – how could the ban not apply to him too, so much younger?

Davey met my gaze. 'You remember,' he said. 'I knew you would.' He let his head fall back against the trunk behind him, his features for once completely at rest.

A longing came over me. To lean back, like him, and let the tree hold us in its heart. Dry and warm in a place no one would ever find us, we could just stay here for ever and ever. But life wasn't like that.

'This is nice, Davey.' I crouched forward on my heels. 'But we should go now. Everyone'll be wondering where you are.'

'No, they won't,' he said. 'They'll know I'm with you.'

The sky between the branches swayed. I sat back, hard against the mass of tree trunk and shoots supporting me. What the blazes was Davey up to? Luring me up here so he could blame the whole escapade on me… Yet why?

'Davey.' I winced at the wobble in my voice. 'We… we made a deal. You promised.'

He pouted. 'Oh, all right. You go first, and I'll follow.'

I felt a smile forming on my lips, in spite of myself. How stupid did he think I was? 'No, you first,' I said. 'I'm not leaving till I can see you on the ground.'

A light entered his eye. 'We'll go together.'

'Don't be silly, there's no room.'

'Me this way' – he clambered across to the V-shaped gap beside me – 'and you take the shortcut.' He nodded over his shoulder to an open area between a cloud of bright green leaves and the trunk against which he'd been sitting. 'Go on – race you!' Slithering round, he climbed one step backwards and looked up at me eagerly.

I wavered. 'There's another way down?'

'You know there is!'

I looked where he pointed, and he laughed in delight. It was a game; all a game! But if that was what it took… Crawling over, I turned, hooked my left arm around a cluster of shoots to support my weight and pushed my feet through the gap.

The light in Davey's eye gleamed stronger. 'Ready, steady – go!' He disappeared from view.

Madness seized me. All I could think was that I mustn't, *mustn't* lose him again. Lunging downwards, my feet met… nothing. No friendly, receiving bough. No foothold. Only empty air. At the last minute, grappling for a hold on the slippery shoots, my right hand closed on a thicker, firmer branch. Kicking hard, I pulled upwards with all my strength, scraping the skin of my chest and my stomach where my clothes had rucked up, until at last I hauled myself back up, heart beating so hard I thought my ribs might break.

I lay, taking great gulps of air, feeling the tree solid under me while my mind turned somersaults. What happened? Did I misunderstand him? Why hadn't I just followed him the way we'd both come up, instead of letting myself get carried away?

After a moment, my heartbeat calmed enough to allow me to crawl to the original opening on the other side of the tree, turn and let myself down. My feet shook as they touched the bough below, but it held safe enough.

I reached the ground ready to throttle Davey. No sign of him. Oh, great. *Now*, at last, having nearly killed me, he'd decided to leave me alone and go home.

Rubbing the bark off my hands, I made my way to the edge of the woodland. My whole body ached and my knees kept locking, as if my legs had forgotten how to walk properly. As well they might, after the shock they'd had. Didn't Davey realise the danger of playing such a trick on me? He couldn't have. It was all a game to him. A game he played with someone called Robin, who knew how to play it without breaking her neck. I didn't. That was the problem.

Crossing the field, I kept my eye on the chapel in the distance and Grange behind it. Any minute now Mr Lockwood, having heard Davey's story, would come striding out, face like thunder, and…

Davey's story. From nowhere, laughter swept through me. Holding my shirt collar tight to my neck, as much to contain the fizzing in my chest as to keep out the cold, I quickened my pace towards the house, a lightness in my step that no amount of slipping in the muddy grass could alter.

Davey could chatter all he liked about his adventure in the woodland with – *Robin*. It was *Robin* who'd be in for a scolding, not me. I never – thank heaven – got the chance to tell him my real name. If I crept back into the house now and changed out of my wet clothes, no one would ever be the wiser. As long as my absence hadn't been spotted already, that was.

Square and silent, Ashstone House rose before me. No sign of commotion, the fluster of people searching, though what I expected to see from out here I had no idea. But nearing the south-east corner of the building, I sensed it: eyes, watching me, from an upstairs window.

Like before.

CHAPTER TWELVE

The Watcher in the Rain

A cold, prickly feeling ran up and down my back. Miss Stalkland – had she been playing the spy, letting me break the rules only to pounce the moment I returned? I thought of her warm brown eyes, the calm reassurance in her voice, even when telling you off, and pushed the thought away. Not her style. Sulky Sal, on the other hand… but today was Sunday, her day off. So that left…

No. Not Mrs Fielding. Please, please don't let it be Mrs Fielding. That would be worse than anything. Risking a glance upwards, I nearly cried out in relief.

Chloe. Of course. Only a glimpse as she pulled away from the bay window, but that was enough. Gazing out at the woodland – as she seemed to spend much of her time doing – she'd probably not even noticed the bedraggled girl hurrying across the grass.

Even so, I pushed open the south door cautiously, wincing at the squelching of my sodden shoes across the hall and up the stairs. At the top, I hesitated. To the left ran the normal route to the dormitory, straight past Matron's surgery; I was bound to bump into Stalkie along the way.

To the right... Fear zinged through me at the prospect of tackling the forbidden corridor yet again. Ridiculous! Hadn't I proved the One-Legged Huntsman was a joke? *A joke.* The memory of laughter in the dark rose up and I forced it away with all my might. That had been Lorna, for goodness' sake, nothing else! No. This was the quickest and safest way to Fairfax. Passing Chloe's and Mrs Fielding's bedrooms might be risky but at least their doors would be shut. Tiptoeing by would take seconds.

Slipping off my shoes, I crossed the landing, gripping them in my hand. Once past the windows, the passage plunged into gloom, made even darker by the time it took for my eyes to adjust. The urge to fly the other way, whatever the danger of discovery, swept through me; but then strips of daylight began to outline doorways along the right-hand side, and beyond them, a bluish glow revealed the bathroom. A dozen paces or so and I'd be there.

I'd just drawn level with Chloe's room when the silence around me exploded. From behind her door came a creaking and a thumping; a striding across the floor so heavy that the boards under my own feet shook. I froze, waiting for the door to be torn open and a Chloe I'd never seen before – distraught, from the sound of it – to find me standing there; but the footsteps receded in the opposite direction.

Hugging the left-hand wall, I carried on, my mind staying with Chloe. What was she doing, pacing her bedroom like that? Did she hate the rain so much? I imagined her sitting on a tree stump in the woodland, sketchbook on knee, dipping her brush into a box of watercolours, eyes screwed up against the sun-dappled leaves of the lime tree. Now here she was, caged indoors by the weather, pacing her room like a wild animal.

Reaching the corner, I slipped round it, heart beating in my mouth. Someone was coming down the corridor behind me. Someone whose footsteps were slow and heavy, whose breathing cost effort. As I stood, not daring to move, the footsteps came to a halt at Chloe's door.

A sharp knocking, then Mrs Fielding's voice. 'Chloe! Stop that at once, do you hear? You'll have the plaster down from the ceiling below.' A pause. 'Chloe?'

Tiptoeing into Fairfax, I changed out of my wet clothes and hung them in the wardrobe. Not the best place for them to dry but at least they'd be out of sight of Stalkie's sharp eyes. All the time, Mrs Fielding's voice rang in my ears, not because I was scared she'd find me – it was Chloe she was after – but because there'd been a note in it I couldn't identify. Anger, exasperation, yes, but something else…

Heading back down by the east stairs, trying not to slip in my damp shoes (they'd just have to dry on my feet, I decided), it came to me, and I stopped for a moment before continuing, more slowly, across the empty dining hall.

Fear. That note was fear. What – *of her own daughter*?

Bedtime that evening passed in a haze of bright lights, shouts and chattering, as first Lucy and Susanna arrived in the dorm; then, clumping up the stairs a couple of minutes later, Lorna and Nina. Already in my pyjamas, I wished they'd all settle down and get into theirs.

Susanna came straight over to my bed. 'Got something for you,' she said. 'Only eat it quick before it melts.' She held out her hand.

I was so tired that for a moment all I could do was stare at the single, slightly bruised chocolate wafer peeping out of its silver-foil wrapping.

'Hurry up!' Susanna hissed. 'Lucy's mother gave us a packet each after lunch. Hey, are you all right?' She peered into my face.

Blinking, I focused on the offered treasure. Susanna had broken this piece off, put it in her pocket and saved it for me all afternoon. That took some doing.

'I'm fine, thanks. Even better for this.' Unwrapping the wafer, I popped it into my mouth.

'You must have had a really boring day,' said Susanna. 'Too wet even to play outside.'

'Not boring,' I said, truthfully, through a mouth full of chocolate. 'Juft... tiring.' Looking into Susanna's large brown eyes, an urge to pour out everything overwhelmed me; but I couldn't, not right now.

Or ever, perhaps. Because if she found the idea of Davey's turning up in the middle of Lorna's pony jumps last Sunday hard to believe, what would she make of his hauling me out of the library, in the pouring rain, just to see some strange, sodden, criss-cross-patterned flowers in the far corner of the games field?

CHAPTER THIRTEEN

Susanna's Story

A glorious sight greeted me as I entered the dining hall for break on the first day of May: among the letters laid out on the tables, not one, but two were for me. Three, almost, because the one from Mum had a PS from Robbie scrawled at the bottom.

I stood, one knee resting on the bench, slurping my bottle of milk through a straw, and read Mum's letter first. Not much news from home. On Sunday Dad had rung from New York to say he'd arrived; a quick call, not to be repeated unless an emergency occurred, because of the expense. 'Just as well,' Mum wrote:

I've no energy in the evenings anyway. Being deputy head isn't nearly as much fun as it sounds (does it sound fun?), and by the end of the day it's all I can do to open a can of baked beans for Robbie and me.

My lips twisted. Typical Mum, determined to make life at home sound as boring as possible, so I wouldn't feel I was missing anything. As if that could stop me! I imagined her and Robbie arriving home after the long bus ride from St Chad's, Robbie bouncing into the kitchen with all the eagerness of a dog begging to be fed; then moments later, the delicious smell of toasting crumpets wafting through the house…

No. I pushed the picture away. *Don't think about it, just don't.* Gritting my teeth, I went back to Mum's letter.

> *Since you've been gone, your dear brother has taken to wandering around complaining bitterly of boredom, and decapitating the daffodils with his football.*

A snort of laughter escaped me, followed by the thought that at least the flowers being so badly treated weren't fritillaries. Which brought Davey's face before me, cheeks creased and eyebrows working wildly at the possibility of such damage, and I didn't feel like laughing anymore.

The letter ended with 'Big hugs from Mummy', followed by a couple of wonkily written lines:

> *I hop you are well. I am all rigt exept feel sick from super. Spam and spinich, yuck. We played Cherton on Saturday and I scored a gole.*

I snorted at the deliberately written 'No love', followed by Robbie's signature. Too much to expect otherwise.

The second letter I almost couldn't open. Which made no sense, given how I'd longed to hear from

Angie, who'd promised to write lots. But I couldn't separate the rounded handwriting on the envelope from the way she looked at me when I told her I wouldn't be going back to West Hill: sad, but with a kind of relief in her eyes. As if, yes, of course she'd miss me but, you know, maybe it would be easier if I wasn't around.

Stop it, I thought. *Just stop it.*

The envelope was small and light, and when I tore it open a single piece of paper from a notepad floated out.

> *Dear Ellie,*
>
> *Great to hear from you. Ashstone sounds fab! And riding ponies, lucky you. Have you got into any teams yet? I have – I'm now in the FIRSTS for netball. I was nervous at first, with Natasha being captain, but actually she's not so bad once you get to know her. Maybe she's growing up!!!!!*
>
> *Have to go now – extra team practice.*
>
> *Love,*
>
> *Angie*

A five-petalled flower and a smiley face, scrawled so quickly that its eyes, nose and mouth were one continuous, loopy line. I'd spent ages drawing me trying to mount Happy, while he sank his huge teeth into my bottom. But then, time was something I had plenty of, wasn't it? Not being a member of a sports team. Or ever likely to be, even one without Natasha for captain. Natasha! How could Angie suck up to her like that, when she knew exactly what she was like? Tears filled my eyes and I scrunched the slip of paper into a ball, squeezing it into the palm of my hand.

'What's wrong?' Leaning on the table, Susanna looked into my face. 'Is it because your parents can't come again this Sunday?'

'Not that.' Blinking, I thrust what was left of Angie's letter into my pocket. 'Just someone from my last school. I thought she was my friend, but… it doesn't matter.'

Susanna opened her eyes wide. 'Why, what did she say?'

So I explained. As the words left my mouth they sounded silly, petty even. Soon my voice trailed away.

'Let me get this straight,' said Susanna. 'Your friend Angie has just got into the netball team, which is captained by this Natasha person. That tells you something, doesn't it?'

'Tells me what?'

'People do what they have to. At least she's writing to you. My friends don't – can't – do that.'

'Why ever not?' I asked.

'Not safe,' she said. 'For them or… or me. We had to leave, you see. That's why I'm here. My father was about to be arrested.'

I gawped at her. The milk bottle began to slip through my fingers and I only just caught it. 'Why?' I asked. 'Did he do something very bad?'

Now she gave a smile, but it wasn't her normal full, happy one. 'No. Back home you don't have to do something bad to be thrown into jail. You just have to be on the wrong side of the government. My father wrote some things the Prime Minister didn't like – about freedom and democracy and stuff. He's a journalist, you see, and believes people should be allowed to vote for whoever they want. Not just for the Prime Minister who's already in power.'

'Well, of course,' I murmured. 'And he was going to be arrested for that?'

'Yup.' Susanna drained the last of her milk bottle. 'Luckily someone warned him. He came running home and bundled Mum and me and my brother Jacob into the car, with whatever belongings we could throw together. Which wasn't much.'

A hand-carved giraffe and lion. A dog-eared calendar, four years out of date. Precious things indeed.

'We drove through the night and reached Tanganyika… I mean,' she corrected herself, 'Tanzania, that's what it's called now. Anyway, we got there just before the border closed. We stayed with relatives for a while but Dad worried we were putting them in danger, so he spent all the money we had on flights to England. He had friends here from his university days, and they found somewhere for us to live. It had to be in London so my dad could work, because that's where all the newspapers are. But Jacob and I hated it.'

Going over to the crate in the corner of the hall, she plonked in her empty milk bottle.

'Why?' I asked, putting my bottle in beside hers.

'Grey. Walls, roofs, pavements, roads, railings, street lights, even the trees and sky – no, *especially* the sky – all grey. And the traffic! In Malawi we could wander all over, see our friends and run down to the market or into the fields. You can't do that in London. I remember Mum taking us to the park, to prove England had grass, just like Malawi; and I looked at this bare patch of earth with its few dusty green-grey stalks and burst into tears. I said England was horrible and I wished we'd never come.'

I thought of the blue skies and red earth and the bright, fresh green grass in Susanna's battered old calendar. How could anywhere here compete with that?

'I made Dad feel really bad.' Susanna headed down the passage to the boot room. 'He started looking at schools for us in the countryside, a long way from London, where the air would be better too. We'd have ended up boarding in Malawi anyway because the senior school was too far away, so it didn't seem strange to be doing it here – and we qualify for some special Commonwealth fund, apparently. That's how Jacob ended up in Somerset and I came here.'

Pushing open the door to the playground, I flinched at the blast of cold air on my face. 'Not the same, though,' I said. 'You must still miss Malawi.'

'Oh, yes.' Following, Susanna closed her eyes. 'The sun, mostly. On my skin. The smell of the ground just before the rain. The frangipani trees in blossom. Driving up to the plateau to look down at Zomba and all the way to Lake Chilwa and the Shire River.' She took a long breath, drinking in a view that only she could see, though to me it felt vivid enough. 'Then when you're ready to drive back down,' she added, 'you can't until the clock by the side of the road shows the half-hour.'

'What?' A shimmer of heat and bright colours faded into a round, flat face with numbers and ticking hands.

'The road is narrow, so cars can only go in one direction at a time. On the hour, you drive up; on the half-hour, down.'

'Clever,' I said. 'Unless you can't tell the time, that is.'

The next few days were the happiest I'd spent yet at Ashstone. Susanna, Lucy and I went around together, and if the way Lucy smiled and bent her head to explain things grated at times, I managed to take it the way it was meant and smile back. Sometimes Lorna let us tag along with her and Nina, to Lucy's delight and Nina's all-too-obvious disgust; but as we were usually part of a whole group of people being organised by Lorna, there wasn't a lot Nina could do.

On Saturday afternoon we played rounders for fun – and it was a lot more fun, not caring whether you hit the ball or not, but just running and running. And weirdly, because I really didn't care, I did hit the ball, sending it far across the grass, and when I finished running everyone cheered because I'd got all the way to fourth base and scored a rounder. Even Lorna called out, 'Well done, Eleanor!', which made me glow inside; all the more, I have to admit, when I saw the expression on Nina's face. And it was just bad luck that, when it was Nina's turn to bat, she hit the ball in a beautiful curve, straight into the cupped hands of Susanna on the fielding side.

Letter-writing on Sunday felt quite different from the week before, with the sun streaming in through the windows to the box garden, and the golden certainty that I'd be spending the whole afternoon just with Susanna and Lucy, as Lorna and Nina had gone out again, collected this time by Nina's mother. Mrs Coates was a tall woman, whose hair, a darker shade than her daughter's, fell in rich waves around her shoulders. Watching her leave with the two girls, I found myself wondering if I could ever make my hair shine and curl like that, instead of hanging limp and straight the way it did.

Which was funny, when you came to think of it, after what happened two days later.

Or not funny at all.

CHAPTER FOURTEEN

What Nina Did

I had no shampoo. Every girl had her own bottle, labelled with her name and kept in a cupboard in Stalkie's surgery. But Mum forgot to pack mine, and when writing home, I kept forgetting to ask her to send it. It didn't strike me as important. It just meant that, for the past couple of weeks, when at lunchtime Miss Stalkland read out my name as one of the girls who were to wash their hair during games that afternoon, I went up to her afterwards to explain why I couldn't.

On Tuesday it happened again.

'Mum will send some very soon,' I promised.

A fine frown creased Stalkie's usually smooth brow. 'Have you written to her?'

'Yes,' I lied. If I got a letter off straight away it would almost be the same as if I had.

Crossing my name off the list, Stalkie headed for the east stairs. I made to follow, when a hand held me back.

'Ellie.' Head on one side, Nina gave me her familiar upside-down smile that wasn't a smile. 'Is that true? Have you really not washed your hair all term?'

'Not yet,' I said. 'I couldn't.'

She thrust me away as if I were something slimy she'd touched by mistake. 'That's three. Whole. Weeks,' she spelt out. 'Ugh, it must feel disgusting.'

'Not really.' Running my hand through my hair, I stalked towards the stairs. She didn't follow. Mounting the steps, I could feel her eyes on my back. Not until I reached the top and turned left into Fairfax did I hear her begin the flight below.

Well, who cared what Nina thought? And anyway, if I changed for games quickly I could write the letter and leave it in the porch for the post on the way out.

But on entering the dorm, the first thing I saw was Beaky perched on top of Susanna's bedside box, ruffling his wings. As I watched, he began to hop around, knocking over the wooden lion and giraffe, before turning his attention to a piece of shiny paper poking out from the shelf below.

'No, Beaky!' I lunged forwards.

The jackdaw flew up in the air just as Susanna returned from the bathroom. 'What's going—' she began.

'Don't send him over here!' Lucy cupped her hand over something on the surface of her box. 'I've just taken off my necklace!'

'Wretched bird,' said Susanna. 'Always poking his beak in where it's not wanted.'

Together we chased him as he landed by my bedside before fluttering to the windowsill, then to the chest of drawers between Lorna's and Lucy's beds, and, finally, out of the door. Lorna, buttoning up her games skirt, looked on in amusement; while Lucy slid her necklace with its horseshoe pendant – bright, glinting gold, perfect for catching a jackdaw's eye – into a box and pushed it to the back of her shelf.

'Thanks, Eleanor,' said Susanna.

'I reckoned it was better to ignore him,' said Lorna, whose bedside box was so crammed with stuff Beaky had no chance of ever landing there. 'He was hardly going to fly off with any of your things, Susanna.'

'He knocked both the animals over,' I said, 'and was about to attack her calendar.'

'Oh, *that*,' said Lorna. 'It's years old; not worth keeping. Lucy's necklace is much more of a risk.'

Lucy nodded, pursing her lips.

Susanna said nothing. Turning away, she leaned down to straighten the calendar on her shelf, a muscle tightening in her jaw.

That did it. 'You're not supposed to bring jewellery to school anyway,' I said. 'If Beaky gets hold of it, you've only yourself to blame, Lucy.'

Lucy glared at me. She opened her mouth to speak, but Lorna got in first. 'Ooh, look at you, Miss Goody Two Shoes.' She put her hand on her hip. 'Want to know why Lucy's allowed to keep her necklace? It's the last thing her father gave her before he died, that's why.'

'Oh.' Hot shame coursed through me to the roots of my hair. 'Sorry, Lucy. I didn't realise.'

'No. You didn't.' Grabbing her jumper, Lucy followed Lorna out of the dorm.

I stood looking after them, unable to move, replaying what had just happened in my mind. *Must I always put my foot in it?*

Susanna held out my games clothes. 'Better hurry up,' she said, 'or we'll be late.'

The 'we' felt like balm. 'Thanks,' I murmured. 'You don't have to wait for me.'

'You just stuck up for me; of course I'll wait.' She watched as I rushed to change. 'Not your fault, by the way,' she said after a moment. 'You weren't to know about Lucy's father.'

'No, but still,' I said, 'I'd never have... When did he die?'

'A couple of years ago. He was quite old, I think. A lot older than Lucy's mother, anyway.'

I nodded. 'So that's why the necklace... Well, I won't make that mistake again.'

No time to write the letter home now. Together we hurried out of Fairfax and made for the boot room. There we parted, Susanna's coat peg being in a different area from mine.

Flinging myself down on the bench, I bent over to retrieve my games shoes from underneath, when a hard, clear voice spoke close to my ear. 'Ellie, get your disgusting hair out of my face.'

I shot up. Nina crouched in a strange position on the floor, arm stretched out for her own games shoes in the rack next to mine, the rest of her body arched backwards and face turned aside, as if trying to pull herself away.

'Ugh,' she coughed. 'Your hair really smells.' Rising, she called across the room, 'Lorna, did you know Ellie hasn't washed her hair all term?'

The chattering around us ceased. People turned to look in my direction. I sat on the bench, hunched over my games shoe so that strands of hair fell across my face, hiding my eyes.

Lorna turned her head. 'Really, Eleanor? That's… yuck.'

The back of my throat tightened. 'I haven't got any shampoo.' I felt tears rising and forced them back. 'My – my mum hasn't sent me any.'

I'd have done better to keep quiet.

'Ooh, poor little Ellikins,' squeaked Nina. 'Hasn't her mumsy-wumsy sent her any shampooey-wooey?'

'Stop it, Nina.' Susanna's face appeared, looking over Lorna's shoulder. 'You're being mean. Not Eleanor's fault.'

'You could always ask Stalkie, you know,' said Lorna. 'She must have some spare.'

I shook my head. If that were possible, wouldn't Miss Stalkland have suggested it by now? I stared down at my hands twisting the shoe, its rubber sole sticking to my skin.

'You mean, you'd rather have dirty hair than ask for shampoo?' said Lorna. Fanning her face with her hands, she backed towards the door. 'Come on, Nina, let's get out of here.'

'Yeah,' sniggered Nina, 'away from smelly Ellie. Hey, that's good. *Smell-y Ell-ie! Smell-y Ell-ie!*'

That name. It tore into my brain, filling every part to bursting. Floor, walls, painted beams, coats, shoes, diamonds of light from the high windows all broke into splinters of blue, brown, black, grey, white, reforming into another changing room, not long and dark like this one but a wide open space ringing with laughter, while Natasha stood her ground, smiling and smiling as she repeated her cleverness, the name so easily coined, so easily chanted, so easily stuck for ever.

Faces rushed past me. Natasha's smile froze as I brought my fist upwards – only suddenly she wasn't there, and my knuckles bashed against something hard. A stampede of feet away from me, laughter and scuffling and a blast of cold air; I hurled myself after, wrenching my body away from the hand pulling me back, blocking my ears to the voice – it should have been Angie's but it sounded different – calling my name. Through the doorway, out into the playground, where a tall figure with long brown hair danced just out of range and my brain screamed so loud I couldn't hear what she was saying but I could see, well enough, her mouth opening wide and closing, her eyes slits of laughter, and I lunged towards her so that she fell back—

That's when he appeared. From nowhere. Head going up and down, eyebrows working, eyelashes all stuck together with tears, sobbing, hands spread towards me, shaking and begging, 'Don't, please don't! They'll send you away again and I can't bear it, *I can't bear it!*'

Somewhere the shutter on a kaleidoscope of images clicked shut. My hands fell to my sides. I stood in the playground of Ashstone School – not West Hill – and there, a few feet away, Davey cowered, crying hard, jerking his gaze between me and… Nina.

The cavern that had opened inside my ribcage collapsed. Looking into Davey's pale, blinking eyes, all I wanted to do was hug him. 'It's all right,' I said. 'I'm not going to do anything.'

'Weren't you?' Nina tucked her hair behind her ears. Her fingers shook slightly. 'Certainly looked like it to me.'

Lorna put an arm around her shoulder. 'That's a nasty temper you've got, Eleanor,' she said. 'You need to get it under control. You can't go round hitting people.'

'She didn't hit anyone.' Susanna came up beside me. 'But it would serve you right if she had. You were being horrible, Nina. Come on, Eleanor, let's go.'

I felt her hand on my arm but I couldn't go with her, not yet. Davey's sobs had died down but his eyebrows still rose and fell, sending wrinkles up and down his forehead. Pulling away from Susanna, I went over to him, crouching down on my heels.

'Don't be so upset,' I said. 'I'm sorry I frightened you. Look, I'm OK now; I've calmed down.' I tried to take his arm.

He shrank back so fast I nearly lost my balance. Head

turned, as if he didn't dare look me straight in the eye, he whispered, 'Don't get angry. If you hurt people they'll send you away. You mustn't let them, you mustn't.'

It felt as if all the breath had been knocked from my body. I got to my feet, vaguely aware of there being more space around me, of eyes staring at us both from further away, but none of that mattered right now. What mattered was, how did he *know*? No one was meant to know, not even Mrs Fielding. A fresh start, that was the deal! For West Hill, for Natasha, and above all for me.

Well, so much for promises. Because if even Mrs Fielding's six-year-old grandson knew my story, then who among the teachers didn't? And the girls – if they didn't know before, they would now! I risked a glance round and saw, with a flicker of surprise, not just a handful of familiar faces but at least a dozen people standing in a circle around Davey and me, their eyes watchful. Catching my gaze, Lorna and Nina stopped whispering. Odd. I expected to see triumph in their expressions. Not something that looked like – fear.

Susanna took my hand. 'Eleanor,' she said, 'you're not well. Come and sit down for a minute.'

'We'll take you to Miss Stalkland.' Eyes unnaturally wide, Lucy appeared on my other side. 'Don't worry about games.'

People fell away as they turned me in the direction of the boot room. Murmurings followed – from Lorna and Nina, of course – but from others too. 'Completely mad… Kneeling down and talking to the air… What on earth's the matter with her?'

I thought *they* were all mad. Couldn't they see I was trying to comfort that poor, strange, distraught boy? Craning my neck to say goodbye to him, I felt Lucy pull me to one side as a figure passed us, much too close. As if we weren't even there.

'Sorry, Chloe,' mumbled Lucy.

I swivelled round, and for a moment Davey, Nina, Lorna and all the staring faces went out of my head.

Chloe stood in the middle of the playground, her long, usually straight back bowed as if under some great weight. Her chestnut hair, normally smooth and shining in its clasp at the back of her neck, hung loose over her shoulders, and her clothes looked baggy, with the skirt zip slipped round to the wrong part of her waist. I realised suddenly that for days – a week, even – there'd been no sign of Chloe at mealtimes, and the thought that someone like her could disappear with no one noticing gave me a cold feeling inside.

But most startling of all were her eyes. As they darted round, looking for who knew what, they seemed to burn in hollow sockets, making her skin look even paler than before. Almost yellow.

'What's wrong with Chloe?' I whispered. 'She looks awful.'

Clearly others thought so too. The playground emptied in seconds as girls slid round her and hurried past us towards the games field. No sign of Davey.

'I don't know,' said Susanna. She'd dropped my arm

and stood staring, like me, at the crumpled-looking figure. 'She certainly doesn't look... right.'

'Forget Chloe.' Lucy pushed open the boot room door. 'It's Eleanor we have to worry about.'

The boot room was deserted. The familiar smell of rubber and dust, warmed in the sunlight, felt strangely reassuring. Sitting down on the nearest bench, I leaned my head back against the wall and closed my eyes. 'I'm OK,' I said. 'You don't need to take me to Stalkie.'

'Are you sure?' said Lucy.

'Yes.' I opened my eyes. 'I shouldn't have lost my temper. But I'm fine now. Besides, I'd have to tell her what happened.'

'So tell her,' said Susanna. 'Nina started it all. We'll back you up.'

'Not Nina I'm worried about,' I said. 'It's Davey.' It was OK. I could talk about him at last. No one could have missed him this time. 'He was upset enough. I don't want him in trouble with his mum when she discovers he's been running wild again.'

A kind of film seemed to glide over Lucy's eyes. 'Davey,' she said, folding her arms. 'I suppose you mean David Lockwood?'

'Well, of course. He likes being called Dav—'

'No. He doesn't. No one calls him that, Eleanor. What is this stupid game you keep playing? One minute you're about to punch Nina in the face (and I'm not saying she didn't deserve it); the next you're down on one knee, talking to yourself as if to someone else, scaring us all witless – and now it turns out you were just *pretending* to go crazy, blaming it all on a little boy who's got nothing to do with any of this. Just like before.'

I looked at her, open-mouthed. I tried to reply but my voice dried in my throat. Turning to Susanna, I willed her to say something, anything, to show she was on my side, but though her eyes met mine, she remained silent. It was as if behind those dark brown irises, she was elsewhere altogether.

I licked my lips. 'He was there,' I said. 'You – everyone – you all saw him.'

'Only you,' said Susanna.

'I think,' said Lucy, 'Eleanor needs a bit longer. I'll explain to Mrs Harris that you're not feeling well, and you can follow when you're ready.' Walking to the door, she opened it. 'Coming, Susanna?'

Susanna wavered. 'I'm not sure we should leave her.'

'Why not? She seems fine to me. I'd say she has quite a knack for getting herself out of tricky situations. We're the ones who'll be told off for being late.'

I nodded. 'You both go.' Then to Susanna, 'I'll be fine, don't worry.'

'Well…' Susanna began.

Marching towards her, Lucy yanked her by the arm and pulled her through the doorway.

The door swung shut, leaving me alone.

CHAPTER FIFTEEN

The Lost Pearl

Heaven knows what Lucy said to Mrs Harris. Nothing remotely believable, by the look in the games teacher's eye when I arrived on the field a quarter of an hour late. For punishment she made me tidy away all the rounders equipment afterwards, thus ensuring I'd be late for tea as well.

I didn't care. Lorna, Nina, Lucy and the others were giving me a wide berth anyway. As for Susanna... Picking up a couple of bats from the grass, I felt my heart give a little leap.

'Mrs Harris says I can give you a hand,' said Susanna, taking the bats from me. 'I pointed out I was almost as late as you.'

Her grin was so infectious I couldn't help returning it. 'There's a word for someone who actually asks for punishment,' I said. 'Massa-something.'

'Yup,' she sighed. 'But I was in her bad books anyway for daydreaming instead of fielding.' Dropping the bats in the box, she scooped up the disc marking first base and carried on to the second. 'I wasn't daydreaming. I was thinking. About… Davey.'

I almost let go of the discs in my hand. 'Oh, Susanna' – my breath rushed out – 'you believe me!'

'I don't believe you saw David Lockwood.'

Inside me something splintered. 'I *did*.' My throat swelled, tears surging up, and suddenly convincing Susanna was the most important thing in the world. 'He was crying and shaking his hands, head and eyebrows going up and down – you know, the way they do when he's upset. No, not like that,' I added, as Susanna raised her own eyebrows, '*much* more. Like this.'

It was only a quick imitation, but I stopped as soon as I saw the look on her face. It was no use. If even Susanna thought I was going crazy…

Then I remembered. The worst part of all. 'Look, I *know* I didn't imagine him. He – knows things. About me.'

Susanna frowned. 'What things?'

I stared at the ground. Too late to take the words back now. 'Why I'm here. No one's supposed to know, not even Mrs Fielding. But… but she must do. That's why she….' I swallowed as the memory of that first meeting surfaced in my mind, my great-aunt's pale eyes resting on me, unblinking, a tremor in the folds of skin round her mouth. 'And she must have told Mrs Lockwood, and Davey overheard, and—'

Susanna's frown deepened. 'Eleanor—'

'I hit a girl, Susanna.' There, I'd said it. 'She… she fell against a coat peg and cut her head open. It was awful, blood everywhere. I never meant... I-I wanted to hurt her' – I gripped the discs in my hands, nails digging into the plastic – 'but not like that.'

'Why did you want to hurt her?'

I couldn't meet her gaze. The back of my neck felt hot, games shirt sticking to my skin. 'That name,' I mumbled. 'Same one Nina made up. She – Natasha – thought it was funny. I... I *was* Ellie, you see. At my last school.'

'Which is why you wanted to be Eleanor here,' said Susanna. 'Not so easy to rhyme.'

'Yes. Natasha used to do it all the time. People told me to ignore her and she'd stop. But she didn't. And one day I just... snapped.'

'You punched her.'

'Yes.'

'Did she have to go to hospital?'

I nodded, mouth shut tight.

'Stitches?'

'No, not as bad as that! They kept her for... for observation or something, overnight, that's all.'

'Mm-hm.' Susanna looked away, chewing her lip.

A silence fell. The plastic discs in my hands felt heavy, weighing me down. Dropping them in the box, I turned towards the house. No point in hanging around anymore. Not now Susanna would never speak to me again.

'So Natasha got a bump and a headache. You got expelled. Doesn't sound fair to me. Are Natasha's parents very important or something?'

'No, not partic…' I began. Then I whirled round. 'You mean, you don't blame me?' Something was happening to the muscles in my face. Laughter or tears, I wasn't sure.

''Course I don't, silly.' Walking over, Susanna let her collection of bats and discs fall into the equipment box. 'If Natasha was anything like Nina, I'd have wanted to clonk her one too. The great thing is, you managed *not* to hit Nina. You've done nothing wrong. Don't forget that.'

'Only because Davey turned up,' I groaned. 'He knows, don't you see? He could see it all happening again and he ran out to stop me.'

'Why would a six-year-old boy come to the aid of an eleven-year-old girl he's never met?'

'But he thinks he has. He keeps calling me Robin; that's why he…' My words dried up. Of course. How could I have been so stupid?

'*Robin?*' Susanna wrinkled her brow. 'Sounds like a boy's name.'

'Definitely a girl,' I murmured. 'Someone who was here before.'

'Not in my time. And I've been here nearly three years now.'

'Mm-hm.' My mind was elsewhere, grappling with the piece of solid logic that had just tumbled into it.

Davey couldn't know my history. Not when he mistook me for someone else. For the second time in three days, a great wave of relief at this unwilling impersonation washed over me. What I'd thought must be common knowledge need never be, if I held my nerve.

Taking my arm, Susanna walked me towards the house. 'Now,' she said, 'let's forget about tea. No one'll care whether we have a glass of milk and some stale cake or not. I want to tell you about my grandmother.'

I nearly burst out laughing. 'To stop me thinking about Davey, you mean?'

'Maybe.' Susanna gave a slight shrug. Her eyes gleamed. 'Maybe not. My grandmother lives in a village, quite a long way from Zomba. We go there often – used to go there,' she corrected herself, 'and she'd give us sugar cane to suck. Afterwards she'd make us chew bark to strengthen our teeth.' Susanna grinned. 'I loved sitting outside her hut, watching her pound dried maize in a *mtondo* – that's a big wooden bowl – till it was fine enough to cook. Then, while she was making *nsima* – a sort of porridge – she'd tell us stories about her childhood. One story got to me so much, I made her tell it over and over. It happened when my grandmother was ten years old, and it was about a little girl called Pearl.'

'Nice name,' I said. 'Sort of shining and soft.'

Susanna nodded and continued. 'While my grandmother worked hard all day at her chores – sweeping the ground in front of the hut, looking after the goats, tending the vegetable patch – she'd often look longingly at the younger village children, who were still allowed to chase around and play. And after a while, Gogo – Gran – noticed a tiny girl, around three or four years old, running with the others all day; but when night fell, they left her alone. Watching her wander from hut to hut till it grew too dark to see, Gogo became anxious: she knew every family in the village and couldn't work out where this girl belonged. So she asked the children and they were baffled; none of them had seen her. Yet there she stood, at the edge of the group, watching my grandmother with big, sad eyes.'

I felt a prickling on my skin. 'What did your grandmother do?' I whispered.

'She went to the *sing'anga* – the medicine man. He listened as Gogo described the girl, and at the end he nodded. Yes, he knew her. Her name was Pearl. Her widowed mother had married a man from another village and left her behind.'

'Oh no, how could she?' I said. 'Her own—'

'Pearl was dead. Buried in the village graveyard, years before.'

We reached the path. Gravel, grass border, earth, and the stone wall of Ashstone House blurred into rough stripes, against which the image in my mind stood out. A slight black girl with cropped hair, barefoot, standing a few yards away, eyes fixed so hard on my face I never noticed when her dark irises changed to blue and her tight brown curls to a shock of fine, pale hair above eyebrows rising and falling, rising and falling...

Moistening my lips with difficulty, I said, 'You think this boy I keep seeing and – and – no one else does, you think he's… he's…' The word caught in my throat.

'Dead,' said Susanna. 'Yes, I do.'

'No.' I shook my head. 'He'd be all shadowy, and glide through walls, and you'd feel an icy draught and be terrified – but he's not like that at all. He's real. He's solid.'

'As Pearl was to my grandmother. Invisible to everyone else.'

'Susanna, I *held* him. I reached out and…' I stopped. My hands hung by my sides, as empty and useless as when Davey shrank away from their touch. Keeping my voice as steady as I could, I said, 'So what could your grandmother do?'

'If the dead don't rest it's because there's something unfinished, some question left hanging in the air,' Susanna continued, turning right down the path. 'Only Tiwonge – Pearl's mother – would know the answer, so Gogo decided to seek her out. Walking a whole day, she reached Tiwonge's village at dusk and found her sitting round a fire with the other villagers. When Gogo explained her errand, Tiwonge's eyes filled with tears. "Oh," she replied. "I wanted to go to the graveyard and say goodbye but there was no time. Chikosi" – that was her husband – "was anxious to get here before nightfall. My poor little Pearl," she added in a whisper.

'The next day, Tiwonge accompanied my grandmother back to her village and went straight to her daughter's grave. "Pearl," she said, "I will always love you. But I don't live here anymore. I am with a good man and have a good life, and one day we will meet again. Goodbye, my daughter." Then she sprinkled powders the *sing'anga* gave her around the grave and chanted some special words, and, having spent the night with her family in the village, left at dawn.'

We'd reached the drive. Tea would be over soon and here we were, still in our games clothes, but I didn't care.

'What happened? Did Pearl hear her?'

'Next day, Gogo had double the number of tasks to do, having been away. My great-grandmother kept her busy sweeping out the hut, fetching water and spreading out maize to dry in the sun. At last, at dusk, she snatched a moment to watch the children finish their play – and there stood Pearl.'

'Oh,' I said. 'It didn't work, then.'

'No, listen. She was about twenty paces away, and the light was failing, but from the turn of Pearl's head, Gogo knew she was running her eyes over each of her playmates in turn before letting them rest on her own face. For a moment they stayed there; then, with a little nod, Pearl disappeared in the direction of the graveyard.'

The hairs stood up on the backs of my arms. 'She was saying goodbye,' I whispered.

'Yes.' Susanna nodded. 'And thank you. Because now she could rest in peace, knowing that her mother remembered her. She hadn't been abandoned.'

Past the porch to the hedge dividing the drive from the playground, through the opening and left onto the path leading to the boot room. Voices rang from the corridor beyond as we changed out of our games shoes, but louder and deeper than these, one word echoed in my ears: *Abandoned… abandoned… abandoned.* A great gulf seemed to open at my feet, on the far side of which stood a slight, solitary, fair-haired figure…

'You think that's it?' I said. 'He – Davey – *died*, years ago, and can't rest because he thinks his mother abandoned him? But… why me? Why does he think I can help him?'

'That's what puzzled my grandmother too,' said Susanna. 'She decided that Pearl must have chosen her.'

Chosen. Silly, I know, but the word sent warmth flooding through me all the way to the tips of my ears. No one ever chose Ellie.

Reaching the stairs, Susanna took them two at a time. 'So what we have to do,' she panted, turning into the dormitory, 'is find out what he wants. Knowing who he is would be a start. Next time he appears, don't mess around – ask him!'

I almost laughed out loud. It sounded so easy. I opened my mouth to reply – then closed it. No need to ask Davey what he wanted. Not when he'd made it so clear, several times over. Not his mother. Not even me. I wasn't the one he'd chosen.

It was Robin.

Next time I saw him, I'd put him right straight away.

CHAPTER SIXTEEN

Dr Rake

Only, I didn't see him. Perhaps my behaviour on Tuesday had given him such a shock he was steering clear of me for a bit. Well, if so, he wouldn't be the only one. I was now branded as the mad girl, best avoided and only spoken to out of sheer kindness by people like Susanna and some of the younger girls, who didn't know any better.

It gave me time to think. It had never occurred to me before that Davey could be anything but a real, live, flesh-and-blood boy. But the fact that no one else could see him, even when he stood rocking and flapping and sobbing in the centre of the playground, changed everything; and even though the thought sent cold shivers across my shoulders and down my back, things made sense now that hadn't before. No need, for instance, to make him into a six-year-old, when from his height and abilities he was clearly older. Or to worry about the Lockwoods' little boy – my something-or-other cousin – running wild round the school grounds, when all the time he was safe in Grange with his sister.

That thought alone felt like the shifting of a great weight from my chest.

As soon as I got the chance, I told Susanna about the lime tree.

Her mouth dropped open. 'You climbed it – in the rain?'

I nodded. 'He led me up there. And, Susanna, it's the most amazing hiding place—'

'You do know it's out of bounds, don't you?'

'I thought it might be, but I don't see why. It's much easier to climb than the cedar and we're allowed all over that.'

Susanna looked at me. 'The lime tree is forbidden because it's dangerous,' she said. 'Mrs Fielding's very strong on that.'

'It isn't, not really,' I said. 'Oh, except…'

'Yes?'

'Well, he did sort of dare me to come down a different way. Which wasn't there.'

'Wasn't *there*?'

'Yeah. Luckily I realised in time. He thinks I'm Robin, remember? It was obviously some game they used to play.'

'Mm.' An expression I couldn't read entered Susanna's eyes. 'You have to tell him, Eleanor,' she said after a moment. 'He's got to understand you're not this Robin person. Whoever she is.'

I felt a spark of irritation. 'I'm going to. But I can't till I see him again, can I?'

'Tell him,' she repeated. 'Don't let him tangle you in any more games. It's really important.'

'All right, all right!' She looked so serious I felt bad for shouting at her. 'Sorry,' I said. 'I will tell him. The moment he turns up, I promise.'

Several times over the next few days – in the dormitory, across the playground, during games, even passing me as I practised the piano in an empty classroom – Susanna caught my eye. Only I knew what that questioning look meant. Each time I answered with a shake of the head, low-key enough for others not to see – not that they were looking much anyway, except to avoid me.

Meanwhile, deep down inside, there grew a small, solid lump of dread. Everywhere I looked I seemed to see Davey's face lit up with a joy that overflowed and ran down his arms, making his hands dance with delight. To be the cause of that joy, however mistakenly, had felt like a secret treasure hugged close within me; now the thought of destroying it filled me with an unbearable emptiness. By the end of the week I couldn't work out why my neck and shoulders ached so much, until I realised I'd been deliberately not moving my head as I walked around, in case Davey really did appear in the corner of my eye and I'd have to face him and do the deed. When he didn't, I felt a glimmer of hope; perhaps my outburst had frightened him away for good. No need ever to break the news. Davey had faded out of my life of his own free will; the best outcome all round. Really, the best.

One problem, at least, I did manage to fix: my hair. When, by Friday, still no shampoo had arrived in the post, Stalkie gave up. Sending me to the cupboard in her surgery, she told me to find a spare shampoo bottle among all the name-tagged ones there. So, while Sulky Sal sat at the table by the window, examining her straight blonde hair for split ends, I searched the cupboard. It took a while, not helped by the glassy eye that fixed me the moment I opened the door, accompanied by thrusts at my hand from a sharp, curved beak. That darned bird got everywhere.

And then on Saturday I had another riding lesson, and I might just as well not have bothered. Not after what that beast Happy did to me. After my usual failure to make him obey any instruction, he waited until I was halfway through dismounting at the end of the ride to give himself a tremendous shake. One foot still in the stirrup, I fell shoulder first to the ground, my fall broken by something soft, squidgy and strong-smelling.

Ripples of laughter ran through the cluster of younger girls around me. I got up slowly, brushing straw from my bruised shoulder and mud from my face, before yanking my fingers away. Heat rushed into my cheeks. This wasn't mud, this soft, part slimy, part crumbly stuff plastering my hair to my skin.

'You mustn't let Happy get the better of you,' Mrs Lockwood called over from the other side of the yard. 'Next time, show him who's boss.'

I nodded, blinking hard. No point in my showing Happy anything of the sort. Not when he knew it already.

Walking over, Mrs Lockwood took Happy's reins and looked at me more closely. 'Are you all right?'

'Fine.' My voice sounded hoarse. 'I'm fine.'

'Better go and get yourself cleaned up. I'll take care of Happy.'

I couldn't get out of the stable yard fast enough. With Happy off my hands I'd gained valuable minutes; maybe enough to make it to the dorm before the end of games brought everyone else up there to change. That way I could wash away all the horse manure before people noticed how perfectly Nina's horrible nickname suited me.

Crossing the empty playground, I turned right towards the boot room and halted. Through the glass panes in the door I glimpsed a number of figures jostling and chattering, many in yellow Aertex shirts, instead of the usual Ashstone white... of course. There'd been rounders matches that afternoon against St Helen's, a school a few miles away; some of the teams must have finished early and were coming in for tea. Older girls, by the look of it; a mixture of my year and the one above, with a high chance of Lorna and Nina being among them.

I thought quickly. Match teas were served in the gloomy, yellow-painted common room opening off the boot room corridor, halfway between boot room and dining hall. If I used Ashstone House's main entrance,

I could avoid the corridor altogether, and make straight for the east stairs.

Turning, I ran the length of the hedge skirting the drive and peeped through the branches towards the games field. Yes! The rest of the matches were still in play. From that distance no one would notice a dishevelled, mud-streaked figure dart across the gravel to the porch leading to the front door.

But rounding the end of the hedge, I stopped dead.

A black car stood in the drive. A man in a suit and a brown felt hat – the kind Dad wore when he wanted to look smart – walked to it from the house, pulling on a pair of pale leather gloves. A prospective parent? Somehow I didn't think so. Not from the way Mrs Fielding hurried after him, clasping and unclasping her hands, murmuring something I couldn't hear.

'Not in the least, not in the least,' the man replied over his shoulder. Getting in the car, he wound down the window. 'Please don't give it another thought.' His teeth gleamed.

Putting her hands on the frame, Mrs Fielding bent forward. 'But I'm so sorry you've had a wasted journey, Dr Rake. We talked about it so much, you know. Such a beautiful place, and all the painting possibilities. I really thought this time she'd…' She broke off. The skin below her chin wobbled.

'That's quite all right.' His voice was like honey. 'Just let me know if she changes her mind. Appleton Mead will be there when she's ready.'

I shrank behind the hedge as the car purred past me. Dr Rake stared straight ahead, his mouth a thin line.

Peering through the leaves, I could see Mrs Fielding looking after him. It struck me how smartly she was dressed, in a navy-blue jacket and pleated skirt, a large brooch at her throat. Yet nothing seemed to fit properly, as if the clothes themselves had given up; and an emptiness filled her eyes, usually so strong and piercing. Watching her from the shadows gave me a stab of guilt, as if I'd caught her with nothing on, and I twisted away. But while she stood there, I didn't dare creep back along the hedge in case the movement betrayed me.

At last came the sound of footsteps turning on gravel, heading back to the house. I risked one more glance – and stayed where I was.

In the porch a shadow moved. A figure, seated on a stone bench, raised her head. I caught my breath. Not because there was anything unusual in Chloe's being there, but because from the tilt of her chin, she was about to say something.

Chloe, who didn't speak. Whose voice I'd never heard. I couldn't miss this.

Clinging to the drive side of the hedge, I crept the whole way along till I reached the gap leading through to the playground. Diving in, I stood tucked away, only a few feet from the porch, the blood rushing in my ears. For a moment all I could hear was my own rapid breathing. Then…

'It's no use, Mother. I'm not going.' Chloe's voice, grave and low, floated into my ear with a softness that couldn't have been more different from her sister's clipped tones.

A heavy sigh, followed by a scuffing of shoes on flagstones, indicated Mrs Fielding sitting down opposite her. 'You made that quite clear,' she said. 'And I think you're wrong. Appleton Mead is a beautiful place. It has the best people, with the most up-to-date treatments—'

'I don't want electric shocks on my brain.'

'They won't hurt – and they'll help you, Chloe.'

'Yes, but how, Mother? To forget him. That's what you want, isn't it?'

'No, dear, not completely. Just—'

'I don't want to forget. It would feel like another betrayal.'

'But, Chloe, dearest, he's not coming back. Don't you think I'd give anything to have him back? We – you – have to get on with your own life, however hard that sounds.'

No reply.

'I thought you had, you know,' said Mrs Fielding. 'After your father died, you… you seemed to reach some sort of acceptance. But something's changed. You've been all stirred up again, almost as if we were still back there. As if it's only just happened.'

A long pause. Then Chloe's voice, so soft I had to strain to hear. 'It has for me, Mother. Every day it happens afresh. Yes, I buried it. For years. But when you bury something it doesn't disappear. It stays there, waiting for you to come back, waiting and calling, and you mustn't leave, you *can't* leave, because of the one time, that *one time* you were really needed and you weren't there…' Tears broke through and she couldn't finish.

I stood, not wanting to breathe. I had never thought a single voice could contain so much pain. That her grief for her lost love could still be as raw as on the day he was killed… yet how could she blame herself? Soldiers died in wars, a long way from home. Perhaps he'd been wounded and asking for her, and by the time she got the message and dashed to the hospital it was too late.

From Mrs Fielding's reply, I'd guessed right. 'Chloe, you couldn't have been there. You know that. You were too far away. Even if you had been, who's to say you'd have made a difference? What happened, happened.'

A brief silence fell, broken only by sobs from Chloe. I imagined her shaking her head, not trusting herself to speak, but holding out against something. What it was, I didn't know, but somehow I couldn't help siding with her.

'Keeping you cooped up here was a mistake,' continued Mrs Fielding. 'No – I know it was your wish, but we should have insisted you took up that place at the Royal College of Art. Plenty of people would have given anything to have been in your shoes. The good thing is, it's not too late. They liked your work twelve years ago and you've done so much more since then.'

The jollity in her voice made me cringe. I could see

what she was trying to do. Unfortunately, judging by her steady silence, so could Chloe.

A rustle of clothes, and Mrs Fielding's voice came again, from a lower position. As if she were leaning across, perhaps taking Chloe's hands, forcing her to look up. 'We've just got to get you right, that's all. You need to get away from Ashstone. A short stay at Appleton, only a week or two, could do you the world of good. Dr Rake is convinced—'

'To blazes with Dr Rake!'

'*Chloe!*'

Shoes scraped on stone as Chloe stood up. 'He doesn't care whether I get to art school or not. He just wants your money. I don't need his treatments, I'm fine here—'

'Anyone can see you are *not* fine—'

'—carrying on painting. Lots of artists taught themselves—'

'Chloe, look at the state you're in! You're not eating, not looking after yourself…' Mrs Fielding raised her voice as quick, firm footsteps headed away from her, towards the front door.

'Mother, how can I make you understand? Even if I wanted to leave, he won't let me!'

'Chloe, dearest, that's just *absurd*—'

A creak of the handle, a rattle of the glass panels in the door, then silence.

My heart beat so loud I felt sure Mrs Fielding must hear it. Sharp twigs stuck into my back and shoulders, yet I didn't dare move; not with Mrs Fielding standing, equally motionless, a dozen feet away.

At last, a low groan. 'Oh dear.' Slow, weary footsteps clumped down the porch, followed by the front door clicking shut.

Closing my eyes, I let my head fall back. More twigs dug into my neck and hair but I was barely aware of them. All I knew right then was that I hadn't been discovered. I was safe.

Except that I wasn't. Voices from the games field drew nearer, accompanied by feet crunching on gravel, making straight for my hiding place. Untangling myself, I ran down the path to the playground, veering left into the boot room. In the corridor beyond I breathed more easily; from the chatter and the clink of crockery drifting from the common room, the first teams were still enjoying their tea. It took less than a minute to slip past the open doorway, into the hall, up the east stairs and into Fairfax, where I could at last tear off my filthy riding clothes. Not until I had the hot tap splashing over my face and head, loosening the dried manure that stuck strands of hair to my cheek, could I think about all I'd just witnessed.

I didn't like the sound of Appleton Mead. Even less did I like the look of Dr Rake. *Good for you, Chloe*, said a voice in my head. *Don't let them send you away*.

Rubbing my hair and face with a towel, I stopped. That voice… I thought it had been my own. Yet into my mind rushed a distraught figure, all arms and legs and thistledown hair, crying and pleading. *They'll send you away again. You mustn't let them, you mustn't.*

I thrust the towel back on its hook with such force it made the threads squeak. This was ridiculous. Chloe's case had nothing to do with Davey. I had to get that boy out of my head once and for all.

CHAPTER SEVENTEEN

Fritillaries

If I could have found a moment that evening to tell Susanna what I'd seen, I would have done.

No chance. The dorms buzzed with the usual pre-going-out-on-Sunday excitement, raised to a new level by one extraordinary event: Lorna and Nina would for once not be going home together. Nina's grandmother in Poole was celebrating her seventieth birthday, for which Nina's parents would pick her up and take her straight there. This left a vacancy for Lorna, who'd spent some days letting her gaze travel around the many pairs of eyes turned to hers, before finally bringing it to rest on Lucy.

Lucy – calm, practical, no-nonsense Lucy – could barely contain herself. Her fingers danced as she undid her shoes and pulled off her socks, all the time watching Lorna to ensure they'd both be ready to go to the showers at exactly the same moment. 'What time will your father come tomorrow?' she asked. 'Will he bring your dog?'

'I expect so,' said Lorna. 'As long as he doesn't bring Algy.'

'Oh, your little brother's not so bad.' Lucy smiled, wrinkling her nose. 'He's quite sweet really.'

'Not when you know him.' Tying her dressing gown, Lorna set off for the bathroom.

Lucy hastened after her. 'I'll keep him amused, then,' she said. 'So he doesn't bother you.'

This was too much, even for Lorna, surely? I looked at Susanna, but at that moment Mrs Fielding's voice rang from the corridor and we hurried to get ready for bed.

When, later, we stood around brushing our hair, Lucy said, 'Susanna, I'm sorry I won't be here tomorrow. Will you be OK?'

I stopped brushing. 'Why, what's happening tomorrow?'

Lorna snorted. Lucy stayed, head a little on one side, looking at Susanna.

'What is it?' I said. 'What's going on?'

'No need to shout, Eleanor,' said Lorna.

'Nothing's going on,' said Susanna. 'Of course I'll be OK, Lucy. What do you mean?'

Lucy's smile tightened. Without moving her head, she widened her eyes and sort of pointed them in my direction.

I crumpled inside. A rawness spread up my throat and I turned away so they wouldn't see my fingers gripping the hairbrush.

'Don't be pathetic, Lucy,' said Susanna. 'I'll – *we'll* – be fine.'

'Sure you will,' said Lorna. 'Just… be careful what you call her, that's all.'

The smile in her voice. I folded my arms to stop the hairbrush flying out of my hand and smashing into Lorna's head. Or Lucy's. I hated them both.

'Shut up, both of you,' said Susanna, just as Mrs Fielding loomed in the doorway, checking our efforts.

That was the only time I ever got praised for mine. I brushed my hair so hard it shone.

Chloe didn't appear for chapel on Sunday morning. Mrs Fielding sat alone in the pew, looking downwards, the light from the chandelier carving deep lines around her mouth. Her hair – grey-white, no trace of blue now – lay flat on her head, curls all crushed together and uncared for. As the organ started up for the first hymn, she pulled herself to her feet with difficulty, knuckles whitening on the front of the pew.

All the way through that first hymn, I couldn't help glancing at the door, willing it to open for Chloe to slip inside. It didn't, of course. I looked around the congregation. No one, either among the girls or the teachers, seemed to have noticed her absence, so perhaps it wasn't so unusual. Yet somehow I didn't think so.

Then, as the service ended and the teachers rose to leave, the door to the Lockwoods' pew opened and a little boy with fluffy fair hair scampered across to Mrs Fielding, throwing his arms around her.

I stood on tiptoe, craning forwards. The mass of people making for the door blocked my view, but not before I'd spotted Mrs Fielding bend and enfold him in her arms, a little boy whose head came to just above her waist. As you'd expect for a six-year-old.

'See?' Susanna was waiting for me outside. 'It's not him, is it?'

'Nope,' I said. 'You were right. Might have helped if I'd caught sight of David Lockwood before.'

'Yeah.'

Girls streamed past us; the smaller ones heading left for the main house, the older ones right towards Grange, half hidden by trees. Webster jumped joyfully between the groups, receiving pats and strokes from all sides. No sign of David and Alice Lockwood. They were probably in Grange kitchen by now, tucking into milk and biscuits.

'Let's not hurry back to Fairfax,' said Susanna. 'We'll give Lorna and Lucy time to get changed first.'

We dawdled on the little mound leading down from the chapel, reaching the drive as slowly as we could. *Lorna and Lucy* echoed in my ears. *Lorna and Lucy*. Not *Lorna and Nina*. It didn't sound right somehow.

'Susanna,' I asked, 'why is Lucy so desperate to be friends with Lorna? I thought she was *your* friend.'

Susanna grimaced. 'She is. But Lorna's got something Lucy wants more than anything in the world.'

'What's that?'

'Her own pony. Several, actually. Her dad has a big

stable with lots of horses. The whole family is nuts about riding. Even Nina keeps her pony there; that's why she and Lorna are so close. And Lucy lives nearby and wants to be part of all that.'

'Oh,' I said. 'I see. Don't you mind?'

'Why should I mind? People go out with different friends all the time.'

'Except for Nina and Lorna.'

'Yeah, well, maybe they should.'

Reaching the house, we walked down the porch and opened the front door. Making our way through the group of girls waiting to be collected by their parents, we climbed the stairs, and just missed being knocked flat by two figures coming out of Fairfax. Something in the way Lorna descended the stairs, looking neither left nor right, and certainly not at Lucy, made me suspect that she might be regretting her choice of companion; while Lucy, glued to Lorna's shoulder, bubbled over with excitement.

'…perfect day for riding; I can't wait… Oh, 'bye, Susanna.' From the lower flight, Lucy looked upwards with an anxious smile. 'See you later, OK?'

'Thanks, Lucy, we'll be fine.'

''Bye, Lucy; Lorna.' My words tumbled uselessly down the empty steps. Mouth set tight, I followed Susanna into the dorm.

'Forget them.' Opening the chest of drawers between our beds, Susanna pulled out shirt, jumper and trousers and began to change out of her Sunday dress. 'We've

142

got work to do. After lunch we'll comb every inch of the grounds till we find Davey, so you can make him understand you're not Robin. We won't stop till we find him. He'll have to show up eventually.'

Would he? Her logic made me smile. Reaching for my own drawer, I stopped still, fingers resting on the handles.

'What's wrong?' Susanna followed my gaze to the painting on the wall directly above the chest.

'Those flowers – I never looked at them before.' From the blue earthenware jug, a cluster of bell-like flower heads rose up on delicate stalks, their petals patterned like a fine purple-and-white chessboard. 'They're fritillaries.'

'Fra-*what*?'

A smile formed on my lips. So Chloe too loved these strange, magical-looking flowers. 'I know where she found them,' I said. 'Davey showed me.'

As Susanna and I threaded our way between all the ball games to the far side of the field, I related what I'd witnessed in the porch the day before.

'Wow,' said Susanna when I'd finished. 'Poor Chloe. That doesn't sound good.'

'No.'

'You know everybody thinks she's insane?' Susanna said after a moment.

'Chloe's been strange for years,' I said. 'You all told me that.'

'No, but this is different. When she turned up that day in the playground, eyes staring, hair a mess... That's never happened before. And did you notice how thin she's got? Her clothes were hanging off her.'

I nodded. So people *did* see Chloe.

As we neared the corner between hedge and woodland, it came again: that prickly feeling down my shoulders and back. I looked round.

'What is it?' said Susanna. 'Davey?'

'No.' I scanned the windows all the way along the house. They looked back at me, dark and blank. 'It's nothing.' I gave myself a shake. No one could see us from this distance.

Turning, I concentrated on the long grass, misgivings growing inside me. No fritillaries. I searched more urgently. If I couldn't prove this part of my story, what chance was there for the rest of it? Would Susanna think I'd made up the lot? 'Please, Davey,' I whispered, 'don't do this to me.'

Then I saw it. Crumpled, the chequerboard pattern barely visible, a single purplish bell dangled from a slender stalk. 'There. That's a fritillary. According to Davey.'

Now all around more came into view, their colours faded, petals shrivelled up. Only Davey knew the moment of full flowering. That was why he'd dragged me over here, two weeks ago.

Susanna's eyes widened. 'Davey knows about flowers? I'd expect Chloe to – she paints almost nothing else – but it seems odd for a nine-year-old boy.'

'Everything about Davey is odd.'

After the brightness of the field, it took a moment for our eyes to adjust to the dappled light in the woodland. Round the bases of the trees, bluebells began to appear; pools of blue and white against their fresh green leaves. Lorna's jumping course still marked the winding path, mainly because it had been repaired and improved: a mass of old leaves, twigs, bits of moss and strands of ivy scraped together to build new mounds. A bunch of younger girls busied themselves in lining up and galloping round.

'Hi, Eleanor, come and join us!' Nicola, a springy girl from my riding group, gave me a grin as we walked past. Then her foot caught in the mound and she collapsed into giggles as leaves flew everywhere.

'Not now,' I said. 'Another time.'

At least this lot knew how to have fun.

Reaching the lime tree, we stood for a moment, gazing up at its branches. Heads back, we walked all the way round, until our aching necks forced us to stop and we leaned against the leafy trunk, eyes closed. No doubt about it. The arrangement of branches offered just one way up or down. The alternative was a fifteen-foot drop.

'Promise me this,' said Susanna on our way back across the field. 'You will not let Davey lead you up that tree again, no matter what. I don't like the games he plays. If they really are games,' she added.

'Susanna, he's a little boy,' I said. 'Of course they're games.'

She stared into the distance, chewing her lip. 'Not necessarily.'

'You think it was deliberate? He *wanted* me to fall down the "shortcut" and hurt myself?' I thought of the way Davey's eyes lit up when he saw me, and felt a spurt of anger. 'You don't know him, Susanna. He's not like that. That's just horrible.'

'Sorry.' With a shrug, she carried on walking.

Something twinged inside me. I ran after her. 'No, *I'm* sorry,' I said. 'It's just—'

'You don't need to explain. Only…' She looked me straight in the eye. 'Be careful. Please.'

CHAPTER EIGHTEEN

Disaster in Fairfax

The thundering on the stairs, we expected that. But something was wrong: too many pairs of feet, and a new voice – younger, brighter – interweaving with Lorna's.

'Please, Gran, there's no need—'

'Ha – you just don't want me to see your pathetic little dorm!'

'Enough, both of you.'

Just as well Susanna and I hadn't started getting ready for bed. We just had time to exchange looks before Mrs Stevenson's squat figure, clad in tweed skirt and padded jacket, appeared in the doorway, Lorna and Lucy behind her. Holding her hand and spreading his feet wide so no one could get past, a boy looked round the room with a satisfied expression.

'Hello, girls,' he said. 'Bit bare in here, isn't it?' Brushing a swathe of hair off his forehead, he flashed us a winning smile.

I did not feel won. Not by a cheeky squirt even younger than my brother. 'Hello,' I said.

'Right, Algy,' said Lorna. 'You've seen Fairfax; now you can go.' She tried to squeeze past.

'Lorna, don't push.' Mrs Stevenson walked into the room.

Immediately Algy dropped his grandmother's hand and ran towards the bed in the corner. 'Ha ha, Lorna – not hard to tell where you sleep!' Launching himself onto the bed, he bounced the giant purple Gonk over to the bedside box. With a crash the plastic horse fell over, saddle, bridle and other pieces of equipment scattering across the floor.

Something between a yell and a sob broke from Lorna. In five strides she reached her brother and grabbed him by the collar. 'You nasty, rotten little—'

Throwing his grandmother an imploring look, Algy burst into tears.

Mrs Stevenson marched over to the bed. Her shoes caught on pieces of bridle, sending them skittering further across the floorboards. Slapping Lorna's arm away, she said, 'How many times do I have to tell you, Lorna? He's only playing. And he's half your size.'

Burying his face in the pillow, Algy squirmed all over Lorna's bed. Dried mud and bits of straw slid off his boots onto the coverlet.

Lorna fell back, arms by her sides. 'Gran, please.' Her voice came out as a croak. 'Look what he's doing.'

This was awful. Robbie could be a brat at times, but *this*… I didn't know where to look. Lucy hovered just behind Lorna, trying – and failing – to reach round and

148

lift the Gonk out of the way, while beside me, on hands and knees, Susanna ran her palms over the floorboards, collecting bits of bridle, reins, stirrups and saddle. Kneeling down, I joined in.

'Now, Algy, stop that, there's a good boy,' said Mrs Stevenson. 'We'll be off now. Goodbye, Lorna.'

Bringing half the coverlet with him as he slid off the bed, Algy threw Lorna a triumphant look and followed his grandmother out of the room.

Lorna bent to pick up the coverlet, her hair falling forward so that it concealed her face.

At once Lucy was at her side. 'Poor Lorna,' she said. 'That was really mean of him.'

Lorna picked lumps of mud off the material. Some had been rubbed into the stitching and wouldn't come out.

'Tell you what.' Going over to the window, Lucy pushed up the sash. 'I'll take one end, you take the other and we'll give it a good shake.' Hands on the coverlet, she put her head on one side. 'All right?'

I looked at Lorna. In her place I'd have wrapped the coverlet around Lucy's neck by now. But that was me. And my nasty temper.

Lorna's lips tightened. Without looking up, she gave a slight nod and took her end of the coverlet in both hands.

'That's it.' Leading the way to the window, Lucy fed the material over the sill and began to shake. 'I see what you mean about your brother now. He's really spoilt, isn't he? Your gran lets him get away with murder. I suppose it's because he's the boy.'

It was none of my business. None at all. But this was going too far. 'So what if he's a boy?' I sat back on my heels. 'If my brother behaved like that, he'd get what for.'

'Oh, Eleanor,' Lucy said over her shoulder. 'You don't understand. Algy isn't just *a* boy. He's *the* boy.'

'Lucy…' Lorna's voice held a warning note.

'So?' I stood up, rubbing my knees. 'You're talking nonsense, Lucy. If Algy were my brother, I'd—'

'Yes, we all know what you'd do.' Lucy swung round. 'You showed us in the playground.'

Like a shock of cold water. I stood, blinking, the floor unsteady under my feet.

'Hey, that's not fair, Lucy,' said Susanna.

'The point is, Eleanor, Algy is the only boy in Lorna's family, so he'll—'

'Lucy' – Lorna gripped the bottom of the window frame through the coverlet – 'I don't want to talk—'

'—inherit everything. House, farm; all of it. That's why Lorna's gran keeps telling her to be nice to him, because one day—'

'Will you *shut up*!'

'—he could throw her out. Sorry, Lorna.' At last Lucy turned back to her. 'But Eleanor needs to know.'

'No. She doesn't.' Lorna yanked the coverlet so hard it flew from Lucy's fingers, the corner catching her face and neck. 'I told you, it's my business, no one else's, and what do you do? You just have to stick your nose in everywhere!' Hurling the end of the coverlet over the sill, she shook it hard.

With a cry, Lucy stepped back, her hand on her chest. The next second she grabbed Lorna's arm. 'Bring it in, bring it back in!' she shouted.

Susanna jumped up. 'What's the matter, Lucy? Are you hurt?'

'Why can't you leave me *alone*?' Pulling in the coverlet, Lorna threw it on her bed. 'You're such a goody-goody. All this "poor Lorna" stuff; you make me sick. I wish I'd never asked you out in the first place. And get away from my bed!'

Voices on the landing outside: Mrs Fielding shooing people in Pym and Verney to the bathroom. We should all have been in our night things by now. But I just stood there, mouth open. Annoying though Lucy was, she didn't deserve this.

Not that she seemed to have heard. Kneeling on the floor, she grabbed the coverlet, turning it over. 'My necklace – where's my necklace?' she whimpered. 'It got caught when you… you snatched the thing away.'

'Oh.' Lorna straightened up.

'It's not there.' Head bowed, Lucy began to cry.

'Perhaps it fell out of the window.' Walking over, I peered down at the flower bed below. Pointless. From this height you'd need eagle eyes to pick out a tiny gold horseshoe on a broken chain among the rose bushes and tulips.

Mistake. Quick as lightning, Lorna rounded on me. 'This is all your fault, Eleanor. Who asked you to put your oar in? As if you'd know the first thing about my brother, or... or my family, or anything! If you hadn't baited Lucy, she'd never—'

'What?' I felt as if I'd been punched in the stomach. 'I didn't bait her.'

'What would you call it, then? All you do is make trouble. First with Nina, then Lucy, then me. We were all fine before you arrived.'

Red-faced, eyelashes stuck together with tears, Lucy moved to Lorna's side.

I couldn't speak. I looked at Susanna. *Please*, I begged silently. *Not you too.*

'Lorna, you're talking rubbish.' Going to the window, Susanna pulled down the sash. 'And, Lucy, it was an accident, for goodness'—'

'*What is going on in here?*' Mrs Fielding stood in the doorway, hair trembling as she glared around the room. 'Bed, all of you, *now*. Why, Lucy, whatever is the matter?'

Long after Mrs Fielding had comforted Lucy, harried us all into bed and switched off the light, I lay staring up at the ceiling. In the twilight slanting through the curtains, I traced the criss-cross pattern of carved wood, as if, by following simple geometric lines, I could somehow straighten out what had happened less than an hour before.

Was it all my fault? For once, I'd felt for Lorna; powerless against her horrible little brother. Yet it had made no difference. For her – and for Lucy, who'd just lost the thing she valued most in the world – I'd always be the wrong person in the wrong school at the wrong time. So much for my fresh start!

Tears filled my eyes, trickling down the sides of my head. Turning, I wiped them on my pillow and watched Susanna's sleeping form rise and fall in the bed next to mine. A flicker of warmth stirred in me. Susanna wasn't like them. She was prepared to give me a chance. At once Lorna's face rose before me, looking from Lucy to Susanna and back at me. *We were all fine before you arrived.*

I pressed my face into the pillow. *Stop it*, I said to myself. *Just stop it. Think of things you can do something about, not the ones you can't.* Lucy's necklace, for instance. I couldn't undo the events that had led to its loss, but I could try my hardest to find it. Tomorrow after breakfast I'd go out and scour that flower bed, and I wouldn't stop until…

No, better than that! I could be up early, before everyone, slip out, find the necklace and drop it into Lucy's astonished hands before she even left her bed. Whether or not I was to blame wouldn't matter anymore because everything would be all right. I could even offer to get the chain mended, if need be. Hunching under the bedclothes, I curled into a tight ball and hugged myself. Oh, if only it were morning already!

Reaching for my alarm clock, I hesitated. Setting it too early might send me out before sunrise; too late, and I'd risk bumping into Stalkie or one of the kitchen staff. Settling for 5.15 am, I slipped the clock under my pillow and let my limbs drift into sleep.

CHAPTER NINETEEN

Who Killed Cock Robin?

Light poured through the coloured glass in the east stair windows, patterning the carved handrail in red and blue. Shoes in one hand, I tiptoed down, sticking close to the banisters where the steps were least likely to creak.

In the hall I paused, ears straining. No sound from above. None from the kitchen, either; nothing to indicate the house waking up. Looking around for the quickest and safest way outside, I decided on the south door. In seconds I'd skirted the tables already laid for breakfast, slipped into South Hall and reached the door leading to the box garden. Turning the key in the lock, I pushed it open.

The morning air felt fresh on my face, the smell of grass mingling with a familiar hint of manure and straw from the stables. Away to the east, the rising sun gleamed in a crack between the distant hills, throwing deep shadows to the right of the long box hedgerows. Slipping on my shoes, I turned left, shading my eyes against the brightness, and followed the path round to the east face of the house, where I scanned the first-floor windows. The corner bay on the far right – that must be Pym. Left of that, the stairs, and then – yes – the three sashes together: Fairfax. Picking my way to the patch of flower bed immediately below, I ran my hands over the rough, prickly ground, turning over clods of earth, twigs, tulip petals and sprawling primrose leaves, examining rose bushes for a glimmer of gold caught on a thorny stem. Nothing. After several minutes, eyes aching and hands stinging, I sat back on my heels. The necklace had to be here somewhere. It just had to.

'You won't find it in the flower bed. It's gone.'

I spun round.

A few feet away, on the other side of the path, Davey sat cross-legged on the ground. The sun lit up his hair like spun gold. Beside him, a brown-and-white spaniel snuffled through the grass; catching sight of me, he stopped still and let out a low growl.

'Don't be silly, Rufus, it's only Robin,' said Davey. 'You know Robin.'

The dog's lips curled. Ears flat, he backed away. *My master may be fooled*, he seemed to say, *but I am not.*

A reminder, if I needed one, of what I had to do. 'Davey,' I began, 'where have you been? I've been looking for you.'

He leapt to his feet. 'Do you hear that, Rufi? Robin's been looking for us!'

Oh, that smile! It got me by the heart. 'Yes, I… you need to know something.' Why was this so difficult?

Davey turned to me, lips parted slightly, as if he wondered what game we'd be playing next.

No game. He had to know the truth. 'Davey' – I swallowed hard – 'I… I'm not—'

'But you're looking for something else too!' he said. 'Don't you want to know where it is?'

'What?' My mind reeled.

'A necklace. You were looking for it, don't pretend you weren't!' He grinned.

The necklace! 'Where? Where is it? Did you take it? Please, Davey, tell me!'

He shook his head. '*Who'll carry the link?*' he murmured. '*I, said the Linnet. I'll fetch it in a minute.* Only it wasn't a linnet, it was a jackdaw.'

'*What?*' My head ached with the effort of absorbing all this nonsense, even while something about it had a familiar echo. A snatch of a long-forgotten song, totally out of place right now. 'What are you talking about?' I said. 'If you know where the necklace is…'

I stopped. One word – the last to leave Davey's mouth – rang horribly clear.

'The jackdaw,' said Davey. 'He was pecking at the flower bed. When he flew away, something gold hung from his beak. They love shiny things, remember.'

That bird! That wretched bird! 'Did you see where he flew?' I asked.

Davey raised his eyes skywards. 'Up there.' He pointed.

No. Oh no.

'The chimney on the corner. He's got a nest.'

Sinking to the ground, I clasped my arms round my ankles and buried my face in my knees. Impossible to put things right now. Why did I ever think I could? Never mind Davey and his dog, or anyone who might come past at this moment. If Mrs Fielding herself had appeared for an early morning walk, I couldn't have cared less.

'Robin, don't cry, oh please, don't cry.' Davey's voice, growing more and more frantic, at last pierced my sobs. 'We can get it back. You know we can.'

I wiped my face on my sleeve. 'Do I?'

'Of course. We just go out on the roof, like we used to. It'll be fun.'

'Just go out on the…' What madness was this?

'Yes, yes!' He nodded, jumping up and down, shaking his hands, every nerve in his body crackling with excitement. 'Come on!' Bounding down the path towards the south door, he called back, 'Stay, Rufus! Not you.'

'No. It's too dangerous.' The space between us seemed to shrink and tighten, pulling me after him. But I wasn't going to be caught again. Rufus, lying some yards away, nose on his paws and growling softly, showed even less desire to follow.

'No, it isn't, not if you keep to the leads. You told me that yourself.'

I did? Of course: this was Robin he was talking to. At the same time, a memory flashed: Dad, holding a window open and gazing upwards. *From the second floor you should be able to get out onto the roof and walk round… You'd have to keep to the leads, of course…*

The leads: flat areas of roof sealed with sheets of lead, strong enough to bear a person's weight. Robbie and I had chased each other along enough castle battlements using these, while Dad, leaning against the tower staircase, wrote notes and sketched.

'See? I knew you remembered really.' At the corner of the box garden, Davey called back over his shoulder. 'Hide-and-seek got a lot more fun once you found the key.'

'The key?' My mind swivelled. It felt like fumbling in darkness. 'To the roof… door, you mean?'

'Well, not to the piano.' Rocking his head from side to side, Davey skipped down the path, singing, 'A door key, not a piano key; a door key, not a piano key!'

'Ssh!' I ran after him, up the steps and into South Hall, while inside I struggled to assemble all these pieces of information into some kind of logical order. If a door existed, it must lead to somewhere you could walk. From what Dad had said, there'd be an area of flat roof between the gables and the glass lantern over the dining hall, from which you might be able to reach the chimneys, one of which contained Beaky's nest. It had to be worth a try.

Davey flew up the stairs, humming a tune. Slipping off my shoes, I tiptoed behind him, shoes in hand, turning left on the landing and following the corridor round. Passing Stalkie's bedroom, I held my breath; at the end of the passage, I ducked into the narrow, cramped west stairwell, hurried up to the second floor, and stopped.

I'd never been here before. A corridor stretched before me, lower and narrower than on the floor below, with pale oak doors showing the dorms where third- and fourth-formers slept.

Several paces away, Davey came to a halt next to a deep-set window. 'Well?' he called back. 'Are you getting it or not?'

I froze, glancing at the half-closed doors, expecting them to be wrenched open by bleary-eyed girls: Nicola, or one of the others in my riding group. No one could sleep through a shout like that.

Yes, they could. A shiver ran through me. I'd never get used to this.

Davey nodded towards the bottom of the window. 'The key, Robin, come on!'

The key… Catching up, I looked. The lowest part of the window frame appeared unusually thick, with a pair of vertical lines, about six inches apart, scored deep into the white paint. Taking hold of the frame between the lines, I pulled, and the whole section lifted on a hinge, revealing a glint of metal.

Davey gave a yelp of delight. *'Who'll find the key?'* he sang. *'I, said Cock Robin. I haven't forgotten. I'll find the key.'* Turning, he sped down the corridor and disappeared round the corner.

'Wait...' I clapped my hand over my mouth. *That's right, yell out loud and bring everyone out of their dorms, in a way no sound from Davey ever would!*

I tiptoed after him, catching up in an alcove set midway into the right-hand wall. There, at its end, stood a door. Thrusting the key into the lock, I'd barely got it open when Davey slipped through and out onto the roof. Following, I screwed my eyes shut at the sudden brightness. Behind my eyelids all was pink, and it was a few seconds before I dared open them again.

From the level of my feet, long strips of glass – thick and greenish in the shade, dazzling in the sunlight – sloped upwards to make a pitched roof, as if a giant had sliced off the top of a greenhouse and plonked it up here, hidden from the ground by the rise and fall of gables. Sheets of lead – just as Dad said – made a walkway about three feet wide between glass structure and gables, pooling into a larger area in each corner. Davey stood, a few paces to my left, looking up at the roof opposite.

Following his gaze, I felt my stomach lurch.

The chimneys were nowhere near the leads. They rose from the tops of the gables, right on the four outside edges of the roof; or, like the one picked out by Davey, along the ridge of the main roof itself. A climb over sloping tiles of at least a dozen feet, then another four or five to the top of the chimney...

I shook my head. 'Forget it, Davey. I can't go up there.'

'Yes you can. Look, there's the nest.' He pointed to tufts of straw peeping from the chimney top. 'And no jackdaw, see? Nothing to stop you.'

I almost laughed. 'It's not the jackdaw I'm worried about.'

'Aren't you?'

'Well, yes, I suppose so, but—'

'So why did you say you weren't?'

'I didn't – I mean, I did, but what I meant was—'

'You shouldn't say something if you don't mean it.' Davey's eyebrows began to work up and down. His mouth set hard.

Something fluttered inside me. 'No, of course not,' I said. 'Sorry, Davey. You're right. It's good the jackdaw isn't—'

'He can't stop you getting the necklace back if he's not there. Can he? *Can he?*' Clenching his fists, Davey stepped towards me.

I fell back. It wasn't the gestures so much; it was the intensity of feeling behind them that scared me. As if Davey himself had no idea what emotion would take over next. 'N-no, of course not, it'll be fine.'

Davey's face cleared. 'Go on, then,' he said, nodding several times. 'I'll warn you if he comes back.'

I studied the area of roof under the chimney. It mightn't be so dangerous, after all. The worst I could do would be to slide back down to the leads again, breaking a few tiles on the way. And the chimney was… what, four feet high? With luck I could tackle the nest from this side and never need to reach the ridge at all.

Be careful. A face rose before me, brown eyes looking into mine; usually laughing, not laughing now.

It's OK, Susanna, I thought back. *This isn't the lime tree with its wet branches. I'll be fine.*

Dropping my shoes, I pulled off my socks. Bare feet would grip better on tiles. I turned to walk round the glass roof, on the opposite side from Davey.

'Not that way!'

I wobbled. *For goodness' sake, Davey*, I wanted to say. *Right, left – what difference does it make?* Changing direction, I padded round while he jumped up and down with excitement, flicking his hands. What a puzzle he was, veering from distress to happiness in seconds – and why the happiness? Why should he care so much about the necklace of a girl he didn't even know?

The roof felt scratchy underfoot. I climbed as lightly as I could, balancing my weight across hands and feet so as not to crack any tile. Behind me Davey began to sing again; not in snatches, like before, but in a clear, thrilling sound that seemed to pierce my back like thin steel.

Who killed Cock Robin?
I, said the Sparrow,
with my bow and arrow,
I killed Cock Robin.

There was something relentless in the way the lines came over and over, the music ending in a question where the words didn't. I'd have turned and yelled at him to shut up, but it took all my concentration to keep my hold on the tiles, and I didn't dare look round.

Reaching the chimney, I grasped it and hauled myself up, still this side of the ridge, face against the brickwork. At all costs I mustn't look over and see the drop below, emptiness gaping between me and the hard tarmac of the playground, and all the way to the stables and fields beyond…

My senses reeled. The balls of my feet ached with the strain of standing upright on a sloping roof. Wrapping my arms around the chimney, I eased them gently up until my nose pressed against the square of bricks at the top, while from below the singing grew louder and louder, ringing in my ears, disorientating me so that I closed my eyes tight, trying to shut out the sound. What did Davey think he was doing?

He's just a little boy, I told myself. *He doesn't understand.*

I pressed my body hard against the chimney to stop it trembling. Holding tight with one arm, I reached the other up, very carefully, over the lip – and jerked it back as pain ripped through my palm. With a scream, I lost my balance, arms scraping on brickwork, the rest of my body slipping round towards the ridge. The singing below broke off into disconnected sounds which for a moment I couldn't identify. Then I did, and it chilled me.

Laughter. Davey was laughing. While distant trees and the wide, empty sky danced before my eyes and my feet scrabbled for a hold. Then, as suddenly as it began, the laughter stopped and silence rang in my ears as I clutched the chimney, eyes tight shut, unable to move, even to breathe.

'Keep still.' Not Davey. A woman's voice, low and close behind me. 'Now. Very slowly, bring your right leg down.'

'I… can't move.'

'Yes, you can. I'll steady you.'

I knew that voice. But I couldn't think how. It didn't match any teacher's.

Gritting my teeth so hard my jaw hurt, I managed to shift my leg a little, then stretch it down.

'That's it.' A firm hand took hold of my calf. 'Now the other one.'

Oh, the feeling of that hand! I almost wept. It took hold of my left leg just as gently, as, with a grimace, I pushed my knee off the ridge and down to join the other one. My arms ached as I relaxed my hold on the chimney and let my body slither down the roof. The sensation of solid surface beneath every part of me felt sweet beyond belief. Touching the leads with my toes, I rolled over, rubbing my knees and ankles with my left hand. My right hand hurt horribly where that sharp beak had jabbed it.

That sharp beak. Belonging to the jackdaw, who'd been there all the time. What was this – another of

Davey's games? Like sending me down the 'shortcut' from the lime tree?

'Thank heavens.'

I looked up. Davey was nowhere to be seen. Before me, in a faded silk dressing gown, brown hair spread loose over her shoulders, stood the last person I expected to see.

'*Chloe*,' I gasped. 'How did you…'

I got no further because Chloe stepped back, her face a deathly white. She opened her mouth as if to speak, but no word came out. Nor did I know what to say. Chloe – sad, mysterious Chloe – had just saved my life; I should seize her hand, pour out my thanks… but I couldn't. Instead, fear curled up me at the way her eyes bored into mine.

'Who *are* you?' she whispered.

My throat felt dry. 'Eleanor Cooke,' I managed to squeeze out. 'I'm new this term. I… I think we're sort of rela—'

'You're Eleanor Cooke?'

'Yes,' I said.

She nodded slowly. 'That explains it.'

'Explains what?'

No reply. Her eyes stayed on my face, though what they saw I couldn't work out, as their focus was far away.

I shifted my feet. 'I'd better get back to the dorm,' I said. 'Thanks for… for helping me down, Chloe.' I winced. Could I do no better than that?

'Wait.' She seemed to snap awake. 'What are you doing out here on the roof? It's strictly forbidden.'

Now I was in for it. 'I had to come up here, I'm sorry. Beaky stole Lucy's necklace, and it was up to me to get it back because… because it was sort of my fault. But—'

'Is this what you're looking for?' Brightness glittered in Chloe's outstretched hand. 'I found it over there. Beaky must have dropped it.'

The earth stood still. I followed Chloe's gaze to a spot a few feet from the door. On the right-hand side; the path Davey hadn't wanted me to take. From nowhere at all, a chill crept over my skin. Blinking, I shook it away.

Handing me the necklace, she asked, 'How did you know how to get out here?'

'Davey.' It was out before I could stop myself. 'I mean, I-I guessed.' I bent to stow the necklace in my pocket so she wouldn't see the colour rising to my cheeks.

'*Davey.*' Feeling behind her for the sloping roof, Chloe leaned awkwardly against it, head down, breathing hard.

I didn't know what to do. Was she ill? In shock? Then I realised. 'Oh no, not *David*, I promise. He'd never come up here. Much too dangerous for a six-year-old.'

It made no difference. Because Chloe never heard. 'Davey talks to you.' Her voice came out hoarse, from somewhere behind the curtain of her dark hair. 'He talks to *you*.'

My mouth, half open, stayed still. Chloe knew about – *Davey*?

167

Then something awful happened. All strength seemed to leave Chloe's body. Sinking to the leads, she wrapped her arms around her knees and rocked back and forth. From somewhere inside her came a thin, whimpering sound.

'Chloe, don't cry. Please... please, don't.' What should I do? How to deal with this grown woman gone to pieces at my feet?

'Of course, he talks to you,' she repeated. 'Why didn't I see it?' Closing her eyes, she let her head fall back. 'Oh, Davey, Davey,' she murmured.

I couldn't contain myself. 'You know about him? Then you must know who he wants! It's not me, it's someone called Robin.'

She stopped rocking. Eyes still closed, she sat perfectly still. 'Say that again.'

'Robin. He wants Robin.'

A slow smile spread across her face, still wet with weeping. A beautiful sight, possibly, but not to someone practically dancing with impatience, like me.

'So who is Robin?' I asked. 'Please, Chloe, if you know, tell me.'

She opened her eyes. 'It's me. I'm Robin.'

CHAPTER TWENTY

Chloe's Story

'*You?*' It sounded rude, blurted out like that, but I couldn't help it. 'You're much too…' I stopped, just in time.

Or not. 'Old?' She smiled. 'I wasn't, twenty-two years ago. When Davey was still alive.'

'Twenty-two years?' The lead I stood on seemed to move under my feet, and I grabbed a corner of roof to steady myself. 'It's that long ago?'

'Doesn't feel that long to me. Not… not when he's still here. I knew he was, I knew it!' Clenching her fists, she darted her gaze into all the corners around us, as if to check where Davey might be hiding. 'Even if I couldn't see him. Mother will *have* to believe me now.'

'Mrs Fielding?' I asked. 'Does she know about him?'

Chloe's gaze stopped still. She turned and stared at me. 'Is it possible?'

'Is what possible?'

'You don't know,' she murmured. 'You see him, and he talks to you, and you don't know.' She paused. Then,

'Davey was my brother. He died when I was twelve years old. Not much older than you.'

Around me, the gables stretched upwards on all four sides. Dizziness swept through me and I sank down on the sloping roof beside her. 'Your brother,' I repeated. 'How… did it happen?'

A silence fell. Chloe looked down at her hands, clasped together in her lap. Her lips moved without opening.

'It's OK,' I said. 'You don't have to tell me. It's just, well, it would help me if I understood what's going on.'

'You're right. You, of all people, should know.' She drew herself up. 'Davey was three years younger than me. He followed me everywhere. Grace didn't come along for another five years, so it was always him and me.' A smile glimmered on her lips. 'He drove me mad sometimes with his tricks.'

'What sort of tricks?'

'Well, for one, he'd wait till I was starting down the passage from my room, then run round the other way and switch off all the lights. He thought that hilarious.'

My mouth went dry. A shiver ran over me, plunging me back into darkness and chill gusts of air, laughter echoing down the empty corridor… Not Lorna, then. As if I hadn't known all along. I folded my arms tight across my chest.

'You have to understand – he was different from other children,' said Chloe. 'If he was happy, or sad, he'd do these funny things with his arms and head—'

170

I couldn't help it. 'And eyebrows,' I broke in. 'But only when he's angry.'

Chloe looked at me. 'You *do* know him.'

I nodded. My throat felt tight, all of a sudden.

'My mother didn't want to send him to school. He wouldn't sit still, wouldn't concentrate. He was only ever happy roaming outside, climbing trees, memorising flowers and plants – anything that grew, he loved – and he was so awkward, and behaved so oddly. Give him a few years, Mother thought, and he'd grow out of it.'

'What about your dad?'

'Away at the war. Fighting in Burma, and didn't come home for nearly two years. So Mother taught Davey to read and write herself – goodness knows how she got him to sit still. Then, the moment I got home from school, he'd come running, Rufus at his heels – oh, Rufus was his dog.'

'A spaniel,' I said. 'Brown and white. With a white tip to his tail.'

Chloe let out a sharp breath. 'Y-yes,' she said. 'That's him. Anyway, Davey would drag me off to the garden or the woodland to play, whatever the weather – we found a way to keep dry, you see.'

I did see. In the woodland, under the thick branches of the lime tree.

'He loved being outside. You couldn't coop him up indoors. He had a hobby horse—'

'And a bow and arrow.'

A chuckle escaped her. 'Oh yes, the bow and arrow! He was a fiend with that. But he explained it was all my fault because of the nickname I gave him.'

The hairs stood up on the back of my neck. 'What nickname?'

'Sparrow.'

Sparrow. Roofline, sky and distant trees vanished as I stood once more in the library, one knee resting on the window seat, turning the pages of a small, battered picture book. A book that belonged neither to Chloe nor to her sister, but to the brother who came between them. Who longed for me to call him by the name written there, and I couldn't because I didn't know.

'He was so gawky,' Chloe continued, 'hopping around me all the time, head going up and down, like a little bird. And he loved the name. That's why he called me Robin. Because of the nursery rhyme.'

I nodded.

'Such a pest,' she murmured. 'Always leaping out at me with his bow and arrow, singing:

Who killed Cock Robin?
I, said the Sparrow,
with my bow and arrow,
I killed Cock Robin.

He thought it a tremendous joke.'

I couldn't help it. My mouth stretched into a grin as the memory rose up inside me: Davey singing that old nursery rhyme while I clung for my life to the roof tiles… It was a joke, nothing more! How could I have imagined anything else?

'I was always Robin after that. Never Chloe. If I ever wrote him anything, I had to sign it with a picture of a robin, or he'd refuse to read it. I didn't mind. I loved drawing robins, even just in black and white. There's something very satisfying about their shape. Round and cheerful.'

Ah. Another piece of the jigsaw. 'Then the fat little bird in the *Flower Fairies* book is a robin, not a sparrow. You drew that. Your Christmas present to him; 1945.'

She smiled. 'So it was you looking at those books. I wondered who'd had them out.'

'Was that… the last thing you gave him?' I ventured.

'Yes.' Her head drooped.

I waited, hardly daring to breathe.

'My father came home from the war. He took one look at Davey, running wild, laughing and nodding and babbling about all the flowers and birds in the gardens, and decided enough was enough. The boy was a milksop. He needed school to shake him out of all this silliness. Make a man of him.' Chloe paused. 'He… he was terrified Davey would turn out to be a conchie, like his brother.' She gave me an apologetic look.

I looked back, waiting for her to explain; then it dawned on me. 'His brother – you mean my grandpa.' My mind turned cartwheels. 'What do you mean, a conchie? Why did he call him that?' It sounded like a kind of shell. I had a vision of Grandpa's long legs curling up in the whorls of mother-of-pearl, his upper body and arms following, till all that could be seen was his watery eyes above the droopy points of his moustache.

'Conscientious objector, of course,' said Chloe. 'He refused to fight in the First World War. Sorry, Eleanor, I thought you knew. That's why the rift in our family happened. Father saw it as cowardice, which it wasn't – and in fact your grandfather drove ambulances for the wounded – but that wasn't good enough for Father. Or his father, for that matter. So any signs of… of softness in Davey had to be rooted out.'

I'll bet they did, I thought. *My grandfather, a coward! What, because he rescued people instead of killing them?*

'He convinced my mother,' Chloe continued. 'Told her she was spoiling Davey. I tried to dissuade them – I knew other children would mock the faces he made, his gestures – but they didn't listen. In the rough and tumble of the playground, Davey would soon learn, Father said. The rough and tumble.' A bleakness entered her voice. 'He had no idea.' She paused.

I held my breath.

'So Davey joined me at Woodbourne school. Lessons were all right – no one dared tease him with a teacher there – but playtime was a different matter. I tried to keep the bullies at bay, but we weren't all let out at the same time. I'd dash into the playground to find a dozen of Davey's classmates in a ring around him, copying him and clutching their sides with laughter. The more they laughed, the more it upset him, and the more his head – and eyebrows – well, you know. He just couldn't help it, no matter what my father thought.'

I sat still. Davey's face rose before me, his eyes, widening and narrowing under his up-and-down eyebrows, looking straight into mine with a bewilderment that made me close my own eyes tight, so tight it almost hurt. Before and behind him, on every side, sing-song voices chanted his name from mouths twisted into grins; then the mouths became Nina's and Lorna's, and the playground a square of tarmac leading to the classroom block, before dissolving into the cold, musty walls of West Hill's changing room, electric light glinting off Natasha's white teeth…

'There were two boys in particular.'

I blinked.

'Douglas and Gregory. They told Davey they were his friends and he believed them – of course he did. Why would they say it if they weren't? He was so happy, and for a couple of days when he came home from school it was all "Gregory this" and "Douglas that". My parents were delighted. Things were working out just as they'd said they would. But I knew those boys. They were not his friends. They'd do things like send him indoors to find something that wasn't there, and then run away. They'd huddle together, talking and throwing glances in Davey's direction when they thought he wasn't looking. Well, he wasn't, but I was. I knew they were plotting something.

'A few days before the end of term, I found out. I, and everybody else. We'd just begun a maths lesson when one of the boys in my class, sitting by the window, gave a shout. "Oh my! Take a look outside, everyone!" Mrs Rivers, our teacher, told him off, of course, but it didn't help. Within seconds the whole class had flocked to the windows and pressed their noses against the glass, giggling. From the looks cast in my direction I knew it had to be something to do with Davey.

'Going to the window, I looked out and… and it was as if someone had smacked me, hard, across the face. There was my little brother, stark naked, tearing round the playground. The rest of his class stood in their sports clothes near the gym, whooping and clapping, while in the windows opposite I could see just about every boy and girl in the school enjoying the fun.

'I raced out of the door, pushing past teachers who were also hurrying outside. I caught Davey and told him to stop at once, but he slithered out of my grasp, panting, "No, no, I haven't finished!" His eyes swivelled past me, as if looking for reassurance from somebody.

'Or some*bodies*. I turned, just in time to catch Douglas and Gregory smiling at each other before disappearing into the crowd. I charged after them, through a blur of laughing faces and figures shrinking away, until suddenly I stood there, arms aching, fists hurting like mad, and Douglas and Gregory lay on the ground.'

I let out a gasp. 'Did you kill them?'

'No. Thank heavens, no. Gregory had a split lip and Douglas gave his head quite a bang coming down. But they weren't seriously hurt. Not as much as I wanted them to be. Does that shock you?'

'Not in the least.'

A gleam entered Chloe's eye. 'Of course. You've been there. In the playground, too, like me.'

Meeting her gaze, I smiled back. No need to reply.

'Neither of us could stay at Woodbourne after that. The headmaster said he couldn't be responsible for such a gullible child.' Her mouth tightened. 'He was right there. He couldn't.'

I nodded. Then I froze. I'd heard this story before. *At my cousin's school they once made a boy strip naked and run round the playground… It was ages ago.*

Lorna. The night she made me brave the One-Legged Huntsman. So Davey's ordeal had entered Woodbourne history, his pathetic tale passed down the years for children to snigger over. I looked down at my hands, clasped together in my lap. Here was something Chloe didn't need to know.

'As for me,' she went on, 'I was a hulking great twelve-year-old who'd beaten up two younger boys. The headmaster had no choice but to expel me. That's what he told my parents.'

Of course, I thought. *That's what heads do.*

'I thought I'd be moved to Middleton High, just a few miles away. But my parents decided I needed a complete break from Davey.'

'So they sent you away.' Away from the brother who ran to her all the time, begging her to play. Far away, somewhere he couldn't follow.

'I didn't want to go. We'd never been apart till then. My mother told me not to worry, Davey would be fine learning at home, like before. But Grace was only four, and Mother had her to think about too. I knew she couldn't watch him all the time.'

Grace? It was hard to imagine Mrs Lockwood – her of the straight back, hooded eyes and crisp tongue – as a little girl.

'He had no fear, you see. My parents didn't realise. I'd done too good a job of keeping an eye on him, staying one step ahead. If we climbed trees, or played on the roof, I could tell when he was about to do something reckless and forestall him.'

'That must have taken some doing,' I said.

'It did.' She gave a wry smile. 'Mother, Davey and Grace saw us off,' she continued. 'Getting in the car with Father, I promised Davey I'd be back soon; he just had to be patient and wait for me. His face...' She broke off. 'He was all pale, with this look in his eyes as if... as if I were abandoning him. And I was, I was!' She fumbled in her dressing-gown pocket for a handkerchief. 'I couldn't help it, but he didn't know that. And what... what broke my heart was the way he waved. Mother had told him to be happy for me and... and that's what he was trying to do. I never saw him again.'

I tried to say something – anything. My throat closed up.

'It happened. Summer term, days getting longer… Keeping Davey indoors was impossible. My parents couldn't run after him outside the way I could. One evening – Monday, the 13th May – they called and called him for supper and he never appeared. They searched till dark and long after, by torchlight, and finally they found him. He was lying under the lime tree. Our special place. Where he'd been waiting for me and I'd never… I'd never…' Her voice slid upwards and she buried her face in her arms.

A long silence fell. Away beyond the roofline, a breeze stirred the topmost branches of a tree rising high above the woodland, its fresh green leaves as bright as they must have been on that day, over twenty years ago. More than a nine-year-old who loved the outdoors could resist.

'Chloe.' I made my voice as firm as I could. 'It's not your fault. You mustn't blame yourself.'

She raised her head. 'Of course it's my fault. If I'd kept under control, not beaten the living daylights out of those boys, they'd never have sent me away. I'd have been there to play with him after school, not left him to climb the tree on his own.'

My throat swelled up. 'Still not… not…' I stammered.

She gave a swift shake of her head, as if to discount my mumblings. 'After that, I couldn't come home. The lawn over there' – she nodded towards the games field

– 'the woodland, the wild flowers along the hedges – they were all full of him. My parents were distraught; all they wanted to do was bring me back, for us all to grieve together, but… but I was very angry with them. I stayed away for a year, living with my grandparents when I wasn't at school. And during that year I decided never to let anyone get that close to me again, so close they became a part of me, because if I did… if I did…' Her voice caught in her throat. 'They'd get hurt. And others. I was dangerous, you see.'

'Chloe, *no*.' I couldn't stop the tears rushing into my eyes. 'It's not like that. You're *not*—'

'When I did come home it was all so… different,' she continued, as if nothing I said counted. '*I* was different. I played with Grace but she was too little to do much and… and it was awful, she'd forgotten Davey altogether. My parents thought it for the best. Nothing of Davey's remained around the house; only a couple of his favourite toys that even my mother couldn't bear to part with.'

'His hobby horse,' I said. 'And the bow and arrow.'

A small cry escaped her. 'Is there *anything* you don't know? Yes, those. And the books in the library. Rufus, of course. He'd come and lie beside me and I'd put my hand out, and he'd just… just rest his face on my palm, and I'd feel the damp softness of his jaw and know he missed Davey as much as I did. Otherwise, nothing. Only the field and the woodland; the places Davey loved. And I couldn't bear to go there. In the school holidays I kept to the box garden and the stables, though I didn't ride much. What I loved was painting. And it was painting that gradually brought me back to him. All the things *he* loved – the trees, the hedgerows, the wild flowers – I wanted to set them down, as closely as I could, because, well, he was there, in them. That probably makes no sense to you.'

I thought of Davey soaked to the skin, dancing for joy in a patch of fritillaries, and those same flowers captured in the picture on the wall of Fairfax dorm. 'No, it does,' I said. 'Your pictures are beautiful.'

'Do you think so?' It was extraordinary how her face changed when her smile returned. 'Mother wanted me to go to art school. She sent my portfolio – without telling me – to the Royal College in London and they offered me a place. I was furious.'

'Why?'

'Because I knew I couldn't go. I told you, I felt Davey everywhere, even if I couldn't see him. I'd left him once – how could I do that to him again?'

'But he was – dead,' I whispered. 'You can't change—'

'—what happened. Don't you think I know that? It's something I can't explain. My parents thought time would help – for them and for me. Time and a project. Ashstone House had always been far too big for us. With Davey gone and Grace growing up, they decided to turn it into a girls' boarding school.' She paused. 'Pity they didn't think of that eight years before. They wouldn't have needed to send me away then.'

181

Send me away... send you away. Words heard all too recently, drawn out in a long, desperate plea. Davey, head shooting up and down, darting between me and Nina in the playground, echoing himself of years before. I swallowed, though my throat felt dry as dust.

'Time hasn't helped. Not for me, anyway. If anything, the sense of him holding me here just increased over the years. But nothing like as powerfully as it has in the weeks since you arrived.' Straightening up, she gazed across the lantern to the gables beyond. 'You know what's happened, don't you?'

I stared down at my hands, watching my fingers blur as they curled round each other.

'He thinks you're me. As I was twenty-two years ago. I've come back to him at last.'

CHAPTER TWENTY-ONE

Chloe is Resolved

'He… he can't think that,' I said. My voice felt hoarse with the effort of convincing myself as well as her. 'You've been here all the time.'

'Not all. It was ages – years – before I could bear to set foot in all our favourite places again. By then, I'd changed. I didn't look like you anymore.'

That brought my head up. 'You looked like *me*?'

She opened her eyes wide. 'Why do you think he calls you Robin? When I saw who I'd pulled off the roof, and found I was looking at myself…' She brought her face close to mine. 'Though now I can see there are differences. Your eyes are darker than mine, and my mouth is wider. But otherwise… You can't see it, of course. But he does.'

Yes, and so did Mrs Fielding. *That* was why she stared at me when I first arrived – and I'd thought it was because of what I'd done, not the way I looked! Laughter bubbled up inside me and I closed my mouth tight to stop it spilling over.

Then something happened that killed the laughter

stone dead. From inside the house came the ringing of a handbell. Seven o'clock.

I leapt to my feet. 'Chloe, we have to go. I have to get back to Fairfax before I'm missed.'

Too late. Faces appeared in the glass of the door opposite. From the way they whipped away I knew we'd been seen; by whom I couldn't tell, but it could only be a matter of minutes before Stalkie stormed out onto the roof.

'Chloe!' I urged.

Chloe made no movement. Hands clasped between her knees, she gazed over the roof at the trees waving in the blue sky. 'This is all so extraordinary,' she murmured. 'We need time to take it in. Decide what needs to be done.'

'But I'll be in huge trouble if I'm caught out here, don't you realise?' I clenched my fists, only to unclench them immediately, as pain seared through the palm of my right hand.

'No, you won't. I'll explain it all to Mother. All these years she's insisted it was my imagination, that grief had affected my mental state, that I needed psychiatric help – and I can show her now she's wrong, she's wrong! *You* can show her. We'll go together.' Rising, she smoothed down her dressing gown.

Cradling my sore hand, I said, 'Supposing Mrs Fielding – Great-Aunt Margaret – doesn't believe me?'

'She will, because your story chimes with mine.' Plunging her hands into her pockets, Chloe set off down the leads and round the lantern towards the door with such speed I had to walk fast to keep up. 'Then all we have to do is find Davey and tell him.' She whisked round. 'You must tell him.'

'Me?' I gaped. 'Chloe, it isn't that easy—'

'Make him understand that I'm here, back home where I belong. He doesn't have to wait any longer.'

Looking into her eager eyes, I didn't know what to say. She made it sound so simple. Yet the sense of unease inside me only grew.

The door beside us crashed open and I jumped.

'Eleanor! And... *Chloe*?' Stray curls trembling from her unbrushed hair, chin wobbling over the collar of her flannel dressing gown, Mrs Fielding looked from me to Chloe and back again. 'Just *what* do you two think you're doing?'

'Oh, Mother, something really wonderful!' Chloe beamed back at her. 'About Davey. Eleanor sees him – he talks to her.'

It was as if an invisible thread holding Mrs Fielding upright snapped. From the neck down, her whole body drooped. 'Oh, Chloe.'

'No, Mother, listen.' Bending, Chloe willed her mother's eyes to meet her own. 'He thinks she's me, you see. Well, look at her.' Putting an arm around my shoulders, she drew me forwards. 'And I was right! He *has* been waiting for me all these years. That's why I couldn't leave, couldn't get on with my life. So all we have to do is—'

'*Stop. This. Now.*' Mrs Fielding hammered each word out like the thumping of a stick. 'This is neither the time nor the place. Why have you brought Eleanor up here? What do you think you're playing at, Chloe?'

'Mrs Fielding,' I ventured, 'Chloe didn't bring me, I—'

'Did I ask you, Eleanor?' Swinging her gaze to me, my great-aunt looked me up and down, horror gathering in her eyes.

I looked down. Lichen smeared my jumper and skirt, showing dark green on my untucked blouse. I tried to keep my hands – dirty and scratched – out of sight, but there was nothing I could do about my bare feet.

The colour drained from Mrs Fielding's face. Muscles moved around her eyes, in which the anger had died; instead, a kind of bleakness flickered through them and a gentleness entered her voice. 'Why have you taken your shoes and socks off, child?'

I gulped. Too late to pretend I'd left them in the dorm; there they lay in a heap behind me. 'S-sorry, I'll get them.' I leapt to scoop them up.

'Did it make climbing easier?'

Cheeks burning, I stopped still, back turned towards her.

'I see. Well, run along now and tidy yourself up. We'll talk later.'

Calm; friendly, even – not the telling off I'd expected! I took courage. 'Mrs Fielding, it's all my fault. I – I was messing around and Chloe found me—'

'Later. Now go.'

Nothing for it. As Mrs Fielding pulled the door to behind me, I could see her profile through the glass, turned towards her daughter. 'Chloe, dearest...'

My heart lifted. Chloe was right; her mother would listen now. Then she'd call for me.

A hand seized my arm. 'Eleanor! Are you OK?'

'Susanna.' The person I wanted to see most in the whole world. 'How did you find me?'

'Not difficult.' She grinned. 'I just followed Mrs Fielding as she came storming through Fairfax. The others would've come too, only Stalkie appeared and shooed them back. Nicola came running in, babbling that you were out on the roof, not realising Mrs Fielding was in earshot. Eleanor, what are you doing up here? And why' – she glanced through the panes in the door – 'with Chloe, of all people?'

'I'll tell you,' I said. 'But not here.'

Back along the corridor, dodging surprised girls on their way to breakfast, down the east stairs, through the empty dorm and into the bathroom – all the way I poured out my story. Susanna ran a basin of hot water while I pulled off my grubby clothes. Plunging my hands in, I yelped. I'd forgotten the jackdaw's sharp beak.

Susanna's jaw tightened. 'You risked your life for Lucy's stupid necklace?'

I felt the colour rise to my cheeks. 'I – I didn't think I was risking it. Davey—'

'Davey.' She gave a nod. 'Another of his games, I suppose. When the necklace was lying near you all the time.'

'He can't have seen Beaky drop it – Susanna, don't look at me like that.' Letting out the water, I grabbed my towel. 'He's just a child. He got carried away.' I headed back for the dorm and clean clothes before she could reply. She'd never laid eyes on Davey. If she did, she'd understand.

We never got to breakfast. Just as we reached the landing, a wave of sound hit us from the floor below – voices, creaking of floorboards, scraping of shoes – and the next moment a great clattering as people bounded upstairs.

'Eleanor! What on earth have you been up to?'

'Thank goodness you're OK.'

'Is it true Crazy Chloe tried to push you off the roof?'

'*What?* No, of course not,' I managed to squeak as Lorna, Lucy and – yes – Nina propelled Susanna and me back into Fairfax, onto our beds, and crowded round. 'Chloe isn't crazy,' I protested. 'She – she's just very sad.'

I saw Nina catch Lorna's eye, and something inside me exploded. 'She is *not crazy*! Look, she saved my life! I was about to slip off the roof—'

A sharp intake of breath all round.

'Slip *off?*' said Lorna. 'What were you even doing up there?'

'I… I…' My mind scrambled for what I could tell

them that was even faintly believable, before giving up. 'Getting this.' I pulled the necklace from my pocket.

Lucy blinked. Her hand shook as she reached to take it from me, and her throat moved as if she were trying to speak.

'Looks like you're as nuts as Chloe,' muttered Nina. 'Risking your life for *that*.'

No one replied. Lorna looked from the little pool of gold in Lucy's hand to my face before running her gaze down the rest of me. 'What happened there?' She nodded at the wound on my right hand, which was beginning to bleed again.

'Beaky,' I said. 'That's why I was on the roof. He got to the flower bed before I did.'

Picking up my hand, Lorna turned it over with surprising gentleness. 'You should take that to Stalkie. It needs bandaging.'

Lucy looked stricken. 'That horrible jackdaw!' She almost spat out the words. 'Eleanor, you shouldn't have – I know I was upset but you shouldn't have taken such risks. You... you could have been killed.'

'Yeah,' said Lorna. 'And I was a total cow to you too. Sorry. That was an incredibly brave thing to do. Don't you think, Nina?'

'Of course.' Nina's shoulders gave the tiniest, most imperceptible shrug. But the smile she directed at me didn't seem quite so curved down at the corners as usual.

Not that I cared. I was dancing on air. I'd hoped to undo the mess I'd made of things; I never dreamt I'd manage to turn them round as fully as this. A great shout of laughter arose within me, threatening to burst out, but instead I let Susanna take me to Stalkie's surgery. There, with much tutting on her side about girls playing silly pranks on the roof, and yelps on mine, Stalkie cleaned and bandaged my hand. Making our way downstairs afterwards, I could feel my stomach fizzing at the thought that very soon now – straight after assembly, probably – Mrs Fielding would take me into her study. I was in for a colossal telling-off, that was certain, but at least she'd know about Davey. Surely, then, the three of us – she, Chloe and I – could sort everything out.

I entered the dining hall. No Mrs Fielding. Instead, Mrs Lockwood took prayers and announced the hymn. She'd never done that before.

Lessons that morning passed with agonising slowness. Teachers saw my bandaged hand and made allowances, but that wasn't what was sending my thoughts out of the window and across the playground, down passages and through empty rooms. Where was Mrs Fielding? And Chloe? Were they still together, talking things over – not on the roof, surely, but in Mrs Fielding's study, to which I'd be summoned at any moment? What could be taking so long?

By the end of the second period, a blur of fractions and maths symbols that wriggled across the page, I could wait no longer. 'Enough of this,' I whispered to Susanna. 'I'm going to see Mrs Fielding. Tell Mrs Lockwood my hand's hurting too much to do English and I've gone to Stalkie. Meet you in the hall at break.'

CHAPTER TWENTY-TWO

The Return of Dr Rake

Slipping out of the classroom, I ran towards the boot room – and stopped. From beyond the hedge came the sound of wheels on gravel. Tiptoeing down the path between the bushes, I peered out over the drive and my heart jumped into my mouth.

The same car; sleek and black and gleaming. As I watched, Dr Rake emerged from the driver's seat – but instead of making for the porch, he shot a quick look round and tapped on the back window. The rear doors opened and two bulky-looking men in long white cotton jackets and dark trousers eased themselves out. At some words from the doctor – what, I couldn't hear – they nodded, turned and sauntered up the drive. One – stocky, broad-shouldered, with close-cropped hair around a bald patch on the top of his head – pulled a cigarette packet from his pocket as he walked. The other – taller, with a long, sallow face and a baggy look round his waist – began to pat his own pockets, as if looking (not very successfully) for his own pack. Passing Grange, they turned right and disappeared among the trees.

Reaching into the front passenger seat, the doctor grabbed a briefcase, slim and official-looking. Tucking it under his arm, he smoothed back his hair, pulled down the corners of his tweed jacket and strode towards the porch.

I didn't wait for more. Only one person could be the reason for Dr Rake's visit, and she'd be the last person to have called him. Tearing back down the path, I ran through the boot room, down the passage and reached the opening into the dining hall just as the doorbell jangled. Shrinking back into the passage, I listened, panting as my breath caught up, for the creak of Mrs Fielding's study door opening, followed by her heavy footsteps across the hall.

'Dr Rake, thank goodness you've come.' There was no mistaking the relief in her voice. But why?

'I came as soon as I could.' The porch door clicked shut. 'I was afraid there'd be a crisis sooner or later.' Dr Rake paused. 'I'm so sorry.'

'We are where we are.' Mrs Fielding sighed. 'I just want it over and done with. And you've come alone; I'm so grateful. Makes it much less of… of a thing.'

A thing? I wondered. *What kind of thing?*

'Well, two recommendations are normally needed' – from the direction of his voice and footsteps, Dr Rake was following Mrs Fielding across the floor – 'but in the case of a genuine emergency—'

'Which this is, Doctor. Chloe is dangerous. To herself and to – to others.'

193

What? I nearly fell over. *Dangerous – Chloe?* Straightening up, I risked a look round the doorway.

Hands clasped over the briefcase behind his back, Dr Rake walked solemnly, head bowed. 'In that case, one medical recommendation will do, at least till I get her to Appleton. She'll spend the first few days there being assessed, and we can review the situation. But' – shifting the briefcase to his left hand, he gave it a brisk tap with his right – 'I need to go through the Emergency Order with you first so you understand what is involved.'

'Of course. Come this way.'

Reaching the bottom of the east stairs, Mrs Fielding turned right and disappeared down the short passage to her study, Dr Rake behind her.

Taking my shoes off, I held them in my left hand and half-ran, half-skidded across the wooden floor. Only one thing mattered: *find Chloe.* Warn her she was about to be carted off to Appleton Mead, whether she wanted it or not. What was Mrs Fielding thinking? Her gentleness on the roof, the warmth in her eyes as she turned them on her daughter, so happy after weeks of misery... and then the next minute, making an emergency telephone call to Appleton Mead, a place Chloe wanted nothing to do with!

The slippery, polished stairs forced me to slow down but once at the top I raced through Fairfax, down the corridor, into the gloom outside Chloe's room and knocked on the door.

'Come in, Mother!'

Odd. She sounded cheerful. Had I misread things? But it was too late to go back now, so I turned the handle.

The door didn't move. 'Chloe,' I called, as loud as I dared, 'it's me, Eleanor. Can you let me in?'

'Oh, it's you! Come on in, it's not locked.'

I tried again; still the same result. What was the matter with this stupid door? Dropping my hand, I hit something metallic sticking out just below the handle.

A key. Chloe was locked in. From the outside.

I felt a spark of anger, quickly smothered by a stab of fear. Now I knew what those men in long white jackets skulking in the trees were for. Between them, Mrs Fielding and Dr Rake were taking no chances.

Turning the key and opening the door took seconds. 'Chloe, you've got to come away. You're in terr—'

'Oh, is it break already?' Seated at the dressing table, wearing a pale blue jumper and grey trousers, hairbrush in hand, Chloe swivelled round. 'Mother said she'd fetch me but I see she sent you instead. So much the better. There's something I want to show you.'

'No, Mrs Fielding doesn't know I'm here. I—'

'She must do.' Chloe frowned. 'You're a bit early, you mean. But Mother won't mind. It'll give the three of us more time to talk. Now' – picking up a photo in a silver frame, she held it out to me – 'have a look at this.'

Time to talk… her words tumbled through my brain, making no sense. It sounded as if a meeting had been arranged that I should know about; all I knew was that any minute now Mrs Fielding might step along the corridor, a smooth-faced man with slicked-back hair in tow, and we'd both be trapped.

'Chloe, listen…' I got no further.

From the black-and-white picture in Chloe's hands, two children gazed out, one behind the other. The girl's arms were around the neck of the small boy in front of her, who stood up very straight, in a smart blazer and shorts, knee-high socks disguising his thin legs, and shiny new lace-up shoes. Clothes all utterly unfamiliar to me; but there could be no mistaking that smile. Or the way the hair stuck up around his head like thistledown. The other figure…

I looked closer. My long nose and pointed chin. My straight brown hair falling forward, the fringe grown just below eye level, which annoyed my mum so much. My smile, even; the lopsided way one eye shut more than the other against the sun. My… no. Not my arms. These were thinner, ending in fine wrists and hands.

'You see?' said Chloe softly. 'Uncanny, isn't it? That's me with Davey. His first day of school, taken by my father.' She nodded to the portrait over the mantelpiece.

Her father. Of course it was. Close to, and in daylight, the full figure of an army officer – broad-chested, strong-jawed, crow's feet at the corners of grey, rather sad eyes – stood looking down at me. Not the young man I thought I'd seen, peeping into the poorly lit room, weeks ago now, who could have matched the lost fiancé of our imaginations. In the past few hours all the pieces of the puzzle Susanna and I had tried to fit together had come loose, rearranging themselves to form a picture we'd never guessed at.

Returning the photograph to her dressing table, Chloe glanced at the clock. 'It must be break by now. Shall we go down and find Mother?'

Oh, help, the time! I sprang to life. 'No. Dr Rake's with her. That's why—'

'Dr Rake? How do you know about him?'

I took a deep breath. 'I know that he's come to take you to Appleton Mead. By force, if he has to.'

'He can't do that. Mother—'

'—called him in. Said it was an emergency. They're in her study now, going through the paperwork.'

'What?' Chloe's cheek turned ashen. Her fingers, gripping the chair back, whitened at the tips. 'No,' she said. 'No. Mother would never do that. She promised never to send me away again. We'll go down now and talk to her, as arranged.'

'She arranged nothing with me.' I felt my chest rising, ears straining for footfalls in the corridor. 'Whatever she said was to keep you here. And' – the memory broke through – 'she locked you in! You said the door wasn't locked, and it was.' I ran to the door. 'Chloe, *look*! The key's not in the keyhole, is it? That's because it's *on the outside.*'

Still Chloe made no move. She stared where I pointed, as if unable to grasp the meaning of what she saw.

What to do? It took all my self-control not to rush to her chair and rock her out of it. 'Chloe,' I said, walking swiftly back across the room, 'you must leave *now*—'

Crack. I jumped. From the window came the sound of tiny pebbles flung against glass.

Chloe leapt to her feet. 'What's that?'

Stepping into the bay, I wrenched open the sash. 'Susanna!' I cried.

'We've been searching for you everywhere.' Susanna shaded her eyes with her hand. 'Lorna looked up just now and saw you.' Beside her, craning their necks upwards, stood Lorna, Nina and Lucy.

'What's happening around here?' Lorna put her hands on her hips. 'There's a black car in the drive, and a creepy-looking man talking to Mrs Fielding in her study – we caught sight of them as we ran past the window.'

'Dr Rake,' I said. 'He's come for Chloe. He's got some sort of…' I scrabbled through my memory for the words I'd heard. 'Oh, yes, an *Emergency Order*. And I can't get her to leave her room and hide!'

Nina frowned. 'Who's Dr Rake?'

'He runs a mental hospital,' said Susanna. 'He's been trying to get Chloe there for ages.'

Lorna opened her eyes wide. 'He can't do that.'

'Maybe he can,' said Lucy. 'It sounds like some special document. Did you actually see this Emergency Order, Eleanor?'

'Of course, I didn't!' I almost shouted. As if this was the moment to be cross-questioned by Lucy! 'It was in his briefcase. That's what he's showing Mrs Fielding in her study right now.'

'What's going on?' Chloe stood at my elbow.

Lorna and Nina looked at each other. 'Watch this,' said Lorna. The pair of them set off at a run across the games field to the corner of the woodland, followed a split second later by Susanna and Lucy.

I stared at their shrinking figures. How on earth was this going to help?

'No!' It was as if a bolt shot through Chloe. Crossing the room, she ripped open the door and was halfway down the passage before I could gather myself together.

I raced after, reaching the south stairs just as footsteps sounded in the corridor from the direction of Fairfax. Down the stairs, two at a time, through the south door and left along the path, across the games field and… ah. Now I understood.

In the far corner, between the hedge and the woodland, four figures jumped around, kicking up tufts of grass. The fritillaries were long gone, replaced by cow parsley and buttercups, yet the sight of even these flower heads tossed this way and that brought Davey's face before me, an anguish in his eyes that mirrored Chloe's.

'You – girls – stop that at once!' she cried.

They did. Lorna, Nina and Lucy stood gasping for breath, while Susanna reached out her hand. 'Chloe, you have to hide. I saw Dr Rake. He doesn't look nice.'

'You saw…' Chloe almost choked. 'I don't even know who you are. Or… or any of you—'

'No time,' said Susanna, tugging at her arm. 'But you must – please – come with us now!'

Lorna grabbed her other arm and together the five of us pulled her towards the woodland. Bright yellow buttercups gave way to bluebells, their leaves crunching underfoot, as we plunged into a darkness filled with the scents of sap and wild garlic. Leading the way through the trees, I felt a weight lifting from my chest. By now Mrs Fielding must have discovered the unlocked door; but it would take ages for her to search the house before turning to the garden. By which time Dr Rake would surely have given up and…

No. Oh, no. Reaching the lime tree, I stopped, clutching the trunk.

The south door. I'd left it wide open.

I peered back at the house through the lattice of leaves and branches. There they were, on the steps, already.

Chloe gave a strangled cry. Falling back against the lime tree, she buried her face in her hands. 'Mother *promised*,' she moaned. 'She promised not to send me away again. Not after what happened to Davey.'

'Davey?' said Lucy. 'David, you mean? What's happened to him?'

'No,' said Susanna. 'She means her brother, Davey.'

'Her *brother*? She hasn't got one.' Lucy looked from Chloe to me.

I shook my head. No time to explain now.

'They're looking this way,' said Lorna. 'Hold still, everyone.'

200

Crouching down, I fought to keep my balance. A breeze rustled in the trees and blew leaves down the path. Twigs crackled as people shifted their feet. Somewhere high above, a blackbird sang.

Lorna groaned. 'Our footprints on the grass. We might just as well have put up a sign pointing the way.'

I leaned forward. Through a gap in the leaves, Mrs Fielding's head appeared in profile as she turned to speak to Dr Rake. With a nod, he stepped back into the doorway while she, jaw set firm, hair lifting with the speed of her step, headed straight towards us. She didn't glance back.

No time to escape. And too many of us to hide. Only one thing to do.

I looked at Chloe. 'Your secret place,' I said. 'Yours and Davey's. No one will see you up there.'

'What?' Chloe stepped back. 'No. Not up there. You can't ask that.'

'Would you rather be dragged off to Appleton Mead?' I hissed. 'Have electric shocks fired through your brain?'

Her mouth seemed to slip sideways. 'You don't understand,' she said. 'I can't. I just can't.'

'Yes you can.' Seizing her wrist with my unbandaged hand, I made her face the tree. 'I'll lead the way.' Reaching for the first branch, I hauled myself onto it.

'Eleanor,' said Susanna, 'I don't think that's a good id—'

A gasp broke from Chloe. 'No! No, you mustn't!'

Her hand clawed my leg as I sat astride. 'You don't know how to climb it, you could—'

'Come and show me, then.' Grasping the branch above me between my left hand and right wrist, I pulled my body higher.

'Eleanor. Please. Stop.' The words came between breaths, accompanied by a scraping of shoes and a rustle of clothes against bark.

I nearly crowed out loud. It was working. Chloe was climbing the tree.

Not a moment too soon. From the third branch I caught a glimpse of Mrs Fielding, now about twenty yards from the woodland, while a long way behind her… I narrowed my eyes. Strange. Mrs Fielding had clearly asked Dr Rake to wait inside. So why was he striding down the path, briefcase under his arm, towards the drive? On the ground below, Lucy bent to peer through the bushes in the same direction. I couldn't see her face, but from the intent way she held her head, the question had occurred to her too.

The next moment, all thought of Dr Rake and where he might be heading slid from my mind as the saplings at the edge of the woodland shook and Mrs Fielding's footsteps crunched on the ivy-covered ground.

Lorna sprang into action. 'Quick, we're building jumps.' Scooping up an armful of broken twigs and moss, she ran under the lime tree and back along the path, dropping her burden as far away as possible. Disappearing from beneath me, Lucy followed suit, and in seconds the woodland filled with the sounds of loud chatting and kicking at the undergrowth; anything to divert attention from what might be happening high above their heads.

'*What* is going on?' From behind the tree, Mrs Fielding's voice rang out. 'Who's that over th... *Lorna*?'

Reaching for the branch above to steady myself, I risked a look down. Just below, Chloe sat motionless, leaning her arm on the bough that held me; a position her body relaxed into as if greeting an old friend. I felt a smile tug at my lips. Then it vanished as, ahead, through a gap in the lower leaves, there appeared a brief flash of blue-white curls above a lavender cardigan.

Beside me, the thicket of shoots and smaller trunks concealing Davey's hiding place stretched up. Finding the V-shaped gap, I pushed through, just as fury broke out further down the path.

'What do you girls think you're doing? Break finished ten minutes ago!'

'Sorry, Mrs Fielding,' said Lorna. 'We got carried away.'

'Forgot the time,' put in Nina.

'We just really, really felt like getting some fresh air,' said Lucy, and I couldn't help smiling at the keenness that must be written all over her face.

Which did her no good whatsoever. 'Don't be silly, Lucy,' snapped Mrs Fielding. 'To your classrooms, all of you, *now*!'

Their feet scurried through the leaves, followed by

Mrs Fielding's slower, weary tread. I waited, not daring to breathe. The footsteps receded down the path and out onto the games field, leaving silence behind them. Closing my eyes, I let my head fall back against the trunk behind me.

The next moment I sensed movement as Chloe squeezed through the gap and let herself down beside me, crossing her long legs. We sat inches from each other, breathing in the smell of leaf mould and bark, invisible from below. We were safe. We could stay here for hours, if necessary. Long enough for Dr Rake and his henchmen to give up and go home.

'Hello, Robin. Have you come to play?'

CHAPTER TWENTY-THREE

The Meeting

I thought my heart would burst open. Davey sat on the opposite side of the tree, legs drawn up, arms around his knees. It had worked! I'd brought them together!

'Not to play, Davey,' I said. 'I've got something to tell—'

A gasp came from Chloe.

Davey's welcoming grin faded as familiar lines appeared on his forehead. 'Not to play?' he echoed. 'Why, Robin? Why?' His eyebrows began to move.

No. I must get in there, quick. 'Davey, listen!' I said. 'Please, listen. I'm not—'

Chloe cried out. 'He's here, isn't he? You're talking to him!'

'Yes.'

Chloe seized my wrist. 'Where is he?'

'Straight in front of us. Can't you see?'

'Can't I see what?' said Davey. 'And why are you pointing at me?'

'No.' Chloe shook her head. 'I see nobody. Eleanor, do something. Make him show himself!'

How could I? 'Davey,' I said, 'listen to me carefully. I'm not Robin. I'm not your sister. My name's Eleanor. Your sister is sitting here, next to me.'

'No.' He shook his head. '*You're* my sister. How can you be sitting next to yourself? That's just silly.'

'This lady,' I battled on, 'you don't recognise her because so much time has passed. She's not twelve years old anymore, she's grown up.'

'What lady?' His eyebrows were twitching in earnest now, chin jerking up and down. Hugging his knees, he began to rock back and forth. 'There's no one here but us. You and me. I thought you'd come up here to play.'

A trembling beside me. 'He can't see me, can he?' Chloe put her head close to mine, her breath on my cheek. 'He *must* now. I am… almost you!'

Her words finished in a wail that pierced me to the core. How could they not see each other? Here at last they sat, face to face, not just in any part of Ashstone but in their own secret hideaway, a place known to no one but themselves – and as far from each other as they'd ever been. What could I do?

'Davey,' I said. 'Chloe – Robin – is now grown up. All these years you've been waiting for her and she's been here all the time.'

'No.' Davey dropped his head and began to moan. 'No, no, no.'

'She has. And' – I glanced at Chloe – 'wanting to see you. Wanting that more than anything else in the world.'

The moans grew louder, forcing me to raise my voice.

'But you can't see her because the only picture of her in your head is from when she was twelve years old and looked like me. So—'

'Stop!' Davey jumped to his feet. 'Stop, Robin, I don't like this game.'

'It's not a game.'

'You're lying! Say it's a game, Robin.' Nodding frantically, eyes distraught, he began to back away. 'Please say it's a game. I won't stay if you don't. *Please*.'

This was unbearable. At all costs I had to keep him there. 'All right.' I leaned forwards. 'It's a game, then! But—'

'Aha.' His eyes sparkled. 'Thought so. Now we'll play something else. Follow me!'

'No, wait—'

A gasp from behind. I looked round.

Chloe sat up straight, staring at her hands folded in her lap. 'Just a game,' she murmured. 'Is… is that what you wanted all along?'

'What?' I said.

She looked at me with a bleakness that made me wince. 'I told you everything,' she said. 'Confided in you in a way I haven't to anyone else, not even my mother. Now it seems all you wanted was a bit of fun.'

I gaped at her. 'No – it's not like that, I promise.'

'Can you swear he's here, then?'

'Yes, he's just over…' I stopped. Around me the bare trunks soared upwards into a froth of green leaves.

She nodded. 'I thought not.'

'But he *was*. Didn't you feel him? Just now, he—'

'I don't know what I felt.' She brushed broken twigs and leaves from her trousers. 'All I know is that you and your friends are very clever. Trampling the fritillaries to bring me after you. Luring me up here – to the place he died! All for a good laugh in the dorm after lights out tonight. "Poor, crazy Chloe, what a fool we made of her."'

Tears rushed into my eyes. I couldn't speak. All I could do was shake my head violently as she crawled over to the gap that led down the tree.

Squeezing between the trunks, she said, 'Crying won't help, you know. Not after this. If anyone's sick around here, it's you.' Her head disappeared and she was gone.

I fell back against the trunk where Davey had sat moments before. Sobs rose so fast I couldn't control them; they racked my body, welling up in my throat. Behind my eyelids all turned black as I jammed my face against my knees, every one of Chloe's words feeling like a cut to my skin. How could she think that of me? That it was all a cruel game? And yet it might just as well have been. I'd thought that all I had to do was bring her and Davey together... and it hadn't worked. I'd failed. Failed spectacularly. And not only them, but Susanna who'd believed in me, and Lorna and the others who'd backed me without even knowing the full story.

I pressed my eyes tight shut to contain a fresh wave

of sobs. What was I even doing up in this stupid, hateful tree? Davey was gone – if he'd ever been here at all. All I wanted was to get out of here and forget the whole wretched business. Creep back to the classroom, make up some wild story as to where I'd been… I'd be punished, but so what? Nothing could be as bad as this. Forcing my eyes open, I stared round at smudges of dark brown bark and pale brown shoots and bright green leaves, whose outlines wouldn't harden however much I blinked. Somewhere among them lay the way down. Yes, here, close beside me…

Odd. The gap on my left stretched wider than I remembered. Well, so much the better. Easy to slip through. Easy to …

From far below, a voice called up, full of light and longing. 'This way, Robin. Follow me!'

I followed. My foot touched nothing.

CHAPTER TWENTY-FOUR

Goodbye, Little Sparrow

'*Eleanor!*'

My arms encircling the trunk tightened. For a moment I swayed, my body half-twisted round, one leg bent awkwardly under me, the other through the gap and dangling in the air. On the opposite side of the tree, shapes and textures that hadn't been there before formed into a face I knew.

Susanna pulled herself through the opening, grabbed her way across the tree and wrapped an arm around my waist. 'Pull your leg up,' she ordered.

Her cheek felt cool on mine. I did as I was told, twisting back into the heart of the tree.

'It's him, isn't it?' said Susanna. 'You were following Davey.'

I looked back at her and couldn't reply.

'I heard everything, Eleanor. I thought you and Chloe might need help, so I hid from Mrs Fielding. He couldn't see her, could he? Chloe, I mean. Couldn't – or wouldn't. And you know why?'

Coldness filled my stomach. Yes, I knew. Of course I did.

'He doesn't want a grown woman in her thirties. He wants you. That's why he keeps sending you the wrong way down the tree. He wants you forever.'

Forever. The cold feeling spread from my stomach through all my limbs. Folding my arms around my ankles, I hugged them tight, cheek resting on my knees, while events of the past few weeks tumbled through my memory.

Susanna had been right all along. Those games of his, those narrow shaves… I'd thought they'd been down to my not knowing the rules; now it seemed there had never been any rules at all. Only one fixed, overriding purpose. I squeezed my eyes shut, trying to banish the horror that flooded my body.

Then they snapped open as, across the games field, a voice rang out. A man's voice; one I knew only too well. Friendly, relaxed, as if its owner hadn't spent the last half-hour on a wild goose chase.

'Ah, Miss Fielding – Chloe,' said Dr Rake. 'There you are.'

One look at each other and Susanna and I were both at the V-shaped gap. Slipping through first, I turned, feet scrabbling for the branch beneath, down that one and the one below, thudding to the ground and up instantly, diving through the bushes – no time to take the path – with one thought spinning through me. Where was Chloe? How far away?

Reaching the games field, I spotted her, standing at the east end of the chapel, looking in the direction of

Dr Rake. With a spring in his step, he walked towards her from the drive. Already he'd passed the cedar.

Standing still. Not running for her life, as she should be. Because it had all been a game, hadn't it? A gaggle of girls scaremongering about her mother's secret intentions; it was all part of the hoax. As if she could be in any danger from soft-talking, creepy Dr Rake! Even if she could hear me from this distance, would she listen?

Filling my lungs to bursting, I yelled, '*Ch*—'

A hand clamped over my mouth. A hand smelling of salt and tobacco, so big it blocked my nostrils as well, and for a moment I couldn't breathe. I struggled and kicked, but an arm held me tight around the waist and a voice spoke in my ear.

'That's enough of that, little girl. You just stay nice and quiet and everything will be fine.'

'Hey!' Susanna shouted behind me. 'Who the…? Let her go!'

The man whisked round, yanking me with him. 'Greg!' he called.

No, not her too! How didn't I see these two sneaking up on us? They must have rounded the woodland from the house side just as all my focus was on Chloe. Fighting the hand over my mouth, I managed to part my teeth enough to nip a piece of flesh as hard as I could. The man gave a yelp, and for a second my mouth was free.

'Run, Susanna!' I screamed. 'Get h—'

The hand slammed back over my mouth. Susanna

stood, eyes flitting from one face to another. Then, as Greg lunged towards her, she turned and ran back through the bushes, her footsteps swishing down the path beyond the lime tree.

'No good, Doug.' Greg returned, breathing heavily. 'Little brat's given me the slip.'

In the midst of struggling, I paused. Something stirred in the back of my mind.

'Didn't listen to Doctor, did you?' said Doug. 'He reckoned there'd be more than one of them skulking about. At least she's out of the way. Just leaves us with this one.' Looking around, he spotted the entrance to the woodland in the corner of the games field and set off, half-walking, half-lifting me there.

I dug my heels into the ground whenever I could, but it was hopeless.

Reaching the path, Doug dragged me down it, all the way to the lime tree. 'Now,' he panted, 'we're going to wait right here till Doctor's finished what he's come to do. Not pleasant, having to section someone, but believe me, it's better all round if it's done in a calm and civilised way, without children like you yelling and causing a fuss. Especially' – he raised his voice as I tried to protest – 'for the patient herself. So you can just stand here' – propping me up against the tree, he finally dropped his arms – 'till it's all over.'

Greg joined him. Close to, Greg's extra four inches of height showed clearly, though there was no doubt which one of them was the boss.

'Please,' I begged, 'let me go.' I jerked my head from side to side, straining to look past the pair of them and through the bushes beyond. As if there were any hope of seeing all the way to the chapel!

'All in good time.' Spreading his arms wide to block me, Doug waggled his own head in crude imitation, eyes challenging mine. Blue, round eyes above teeth that glinted and grinned. 'This is fun,' he said.

I hated him.

'Can you do it the other way, too? Like this?' He nodded, hard, chin going right down, then up high, eyebrows bending and rising, sending wrinkles all the way up to what had once been his hairline.

Chin. Eyebrows.

I stood with my back against the lime tree, fingers gripping the bark, unable to move.

'We knew a kid once who used to do that, didn't we, Greg? Skinny, gawky thing. Bit younger than y—'

'*You.*' The word rasped my throat; I could barely speak. Doug and Greg. Douglas and Gregory. Now I knew where I'd heard those names before.

I launched myself at Doug, still standing with arms outstretched, face turned to his friend, and slammed him in the midriff with my balled fist. Pain zigzagged through my bandaged palm, but I didn't care. It was enough to see Doug stumble, thrown off balance, his arms falling instinctively across his body while I shot past.

A bellow erupted from him. 'Why, you…'

I charged through the bushes, ducking under low branches, and out onto the games field. Judging by the explosion of oaths and crashing sounds behind me, Doug and Greg had attempted to follow – as I'd hoped they would – only to find themselves tangled in twigs and briars. With luck, I had a few minutes' start.

I tore across the grass, heart thumping, lungs pumping, a stitch stabbing my side so that I longed to stop, but I didn't dare, and didn't dare look round. Doug and Greg must have regained the path out of the woodland and be on my trail by now; how close I couldn't tell, because the blood rushed in my ears so loud it blotted out everything else.

Ahead of me and gradually growing bigger, the chapel... and yes, they were still there! Hands behind his back, bending from the waist, Dr Rake looked as if he were reading something – what, a gravestone? Could be. I'd never explored that side of the building. Beside him stood Chloe, looking down at his profile, a softness in her expression I recognised only too well. *No*, I wanted to cry, *don't trust him, Chloe! Wait...*

The ground shook under my feet. I risked a look round. Twenty yards behind, two hefty figures pounded across the grass, the corners of their white jackets flapping, their faces red and shiny. Pain zipped through my legs as I forced them on, faster, faster, while ahead, the doctor straightened up, took Chloe's arm and began to lead her along the chapel wall towards the drive. Nor did he seem bothered when she instantly slid her own arm away. His lips moved easily, breaking off every now and then to turn to the tall, silent figure beside him. Little by little, his pace quickened.

And I was barely halfway across the field! Would my cry reach her from this distance? 'Chloe! *Stop!*' I waved my arms in the air.

She heard. Drawing level with the cedar, she turned her head as if to look past the doctor and across the games field; but he manoeuvred her so that the tree blocked her view. He must have taken her arm again because now, beyond the cedar, the two of them appeared to move as one, hastening down the slope towards the drive… where a solitary, white-haired figure in a lavender cardigan stood beside the sleek black car.

Chloe stopped dead. At last she seemed to grasp the danger she was in. Her body leaned at a sharp angle as she tried to pull away, feet fighting the ground, while Dr Rake forced her onwards.

My breath came in short gasps. My legs couldn't take any more. From somewhere a long way back – beyond the heavy footsteps now close behind me – came a thudding, hammering sound I couldn't place. The cedar loomed between me and the drive; already only the top halves of the two figures ahead of me remained visible. Soon I'd lose sight of Chloe altogether. Summoning all my breath, I opened my mouth wide to cry out one last time and …

Oof. My feet went from under me. Pain banged in my chest as I hit the ground. Earth and cedar needles filled my mouth and prickled my nose so that I struggled to breathe. Wrenching my face to the side against the pressure of two pairs of strong arms, I spluttered, 'Let go!'

'Not this time, duckie.' A blast of hot, tobacco-soured breath rushed across my cheek as Doug locked my arm behind my back. 'You want to play nasty, so can w... What the heck?'

My arm was released like a spring. A roar filled my ears: people shouting, shoes scuffing grass, the sound of cotton ripping mixed with yells and grunts from Doug and Greg. I sat up, spitting out cedar needles, to see a whirl of bare arms and legs sticking out from white Aertex shirts and blue games skirts, thumping, pulling, hitting and kicking my persecutors in the softest parts of their bodies, wherever they could reach.

'*Susanna!*' I cried.

Arms around Greg's neck, piggyback style, Susanna grinned at me. 'It was time for gym,' she panted. 'I thought I'd bring everyone here instead.'

'Ow. Ger*roff*.' Eyes shut, Greg fought to loosen Susanna's arms. Raising her knee, Nina gave him a dead leg and he collapsed a few paces away from Doug, who had already been brought down by Lorna, Lucy and several other girls. Reaching around, Doug tried to grab their legs, but they jumped away, shrieking.

Disentangling herself from Greg, Susanna grabbed my hand, pulling me to my feet. 'Let's go,' she said.

Legs aching, knees threatening to give way, I stumbled

round the cedar tree and the last few yards down to the drive, just in time to see Chloe, arm outstretched, pulling back from Dr Rake's grip.

'For the last time,' she said, her voice rising, 'I am *not* going to Appleton Mead. Mother,' she called across the bonnet of the car, 'tell him!'

But Mrs Fielding's attention was all on the cedar. 'What's going on over there?'

Brushing hair out of their eyes, bent double with laughter, a crowd of girls spilled out either side of the trunk.

Mrs Fielding marched towards them. '*What* is the meaning of this *disgraceful*…' She broke off.

From behind the girls, Doug emerged, red-faced, panting, hair bent the wrong way around his bald patch. He was followed by Greg. Crisp white jackets creased and stained with grass and mud, pieces of material flapping where pockets had been torn away, they stood blinking, like huge sea creatures hauled out of their familiar element to flail about on dry land. I couldn't help it; I bent my head to hide a snort of laughter.

An oath broke from Dr Rake, bitten back by a smile, as Mrs Fielding rounded on him.

'Are these men with you, Doctor?' she demanded.

'Mother!' Mrs Lockwood emerged from the opening in the hedge opposite and crunched across the gravel. 'I have 5A in the middle of a spelling test and Mrs Harris has called me out because her gym class…' She stopped. Taking in the whole scene, from Mrs Fielding hovering by the car, to the unruly crowd by the cedar tree, to Dr Rake – one hand clamped on Chloe's wrist, the other signalling quietly to Doug and Greg – she raised her eyebrows so high that for once her eyes shone out beneath them, clear and hard. 'What is this?' she asked. 'Why is Dr Rake holding Chloe like that?'

Mrs Fielding drew herself up. 'My decision, Grace.'

'Mother, Chloe is my *sister.* You do not pack her off to Appleton Mead without telling me.'

'Not in the normal course of things, no. But in an emergency—'

'A what?' said Chloe.

'Chloe, dearest' – Mrs Fielding's gaze swivelled between her daughters – 'I can't take the risk anymore. Not when it comes to putting a pupil's life in danger.'

Chloe reeled as if struck. 'I? *I've* put a pupil's life in...' Her words trailed away as she looked at me.

Understanding ripped through me, sending other thoughts spinning in all directions. This was my fault! *I'd* brought *Chloe* up onto the roof, not the other way round; yet here was Mrs Fielding getting everything wrong, confirming Chloe in her worst fears: that she was dangerous, that the smiling Dr Rake had to be called to take her away, now, *now*, with no chance of explanation!

This was unbearable. 'That's not what happened!' I burst out. 'It was Davey!' Now they'd think *I* was mad, but that couldn't be helped. '*Davey* made me climb onto the roof, not Chloe. She found me and saved my life. Chloe saved me!'

It was like talking into the wind.

'She is *not dangerous*!' My voice rose to a yell but I was past caring. 'If anyone around here needs locking up, it's Dr Rake—'

The smile on the doctor's lips cracked. 'Now, wait a minute—'

'—for setting this couple of toughs on me.' I pointed at Doug and Greg, who looked as if they'd rather be anywhere else than here, right now. 'That's it – grown men attacking children! They're his henchmen! Extra backing to make sure of getting Chloe into his car.'

That, at least, Mrs Fielding heard. 'Is this true? Dr Rake, you gave me your solemn promise that no force would be used.'

For a moment the doctor seemed caught off guard. Then, straightening his shoulders, he smoothed down his tie. 'Mr Reece and Mr Lundy are nursing assistants, Mrs Fielding. I thought it advisable—'

'*Nursing assistants?*' I couldn't believe what I was hearing. 'You mean they look after your patients at Appleton Mead? Chloe would be in the hands of Doug and Greg – or *Douglas and Gregory*, as they were known at Woodbourne School?'

An explosion from Doug behind me. 'How do you know where we went to school?'

'We're only doing our jobs,' whined Greg.

A cry broke from Chloe. For the first time she looked at the two dishevelled men standing there, from the pale, scared eyes of the taller one to the round, pudgy face of the shorter one; then, yanking her arm away from the doctor's, she spoke, eyes blazing. 'You'd leave me with *them*? These two? The thugs who tormented my brother till he died?'

'*What?*' Greg started forwards. 'Who the heck was your brother? We never knew him.'

Doug shot out a restraining hand. 'It's OK, she's insane. It's all coming out now.'

'Oh yes, you did,' I said. 'You showed me. You did an impression of him, over there, in the woodland, remember? Twenty years later and you still find him funny.'

A low moan came from beyond the car as Mrs Fielding buried her face in her hands. Reaching her side, Mrs Lockwood put an arm around her shoulders.

A dull flush appeared on Doug's thick neck, spreading up to his face. His mouth opened and shut like a fish's.

'You… *devils*.' Chloe brought out the words with difficulty, as if they hurt her throat. Fists clenched, she crossed the drive and made straight for the two men.

Alarm flitted across Susanna's face as her eyes locked on mine. The group of girls – no longer laughing – shrank back. From the corner of my eye I glimpsed Dr Rake. Arms folded, legs crossed, he leaned back against his car, a watchful expression on his face.

I ran after Chloe and grabbed her right arm. 'Don't. You're playing into his hands, can't you see? You'll just *prove* you're crazy.'

221

No reply. She tried to shake me off but I clung on, pulling her back, pleading until tears stung my eyes, imprisoning her arm between my left hand and right wrist, dreading the moment when she'd break into wild, fist-flailing, bone-crunching action. Summoning every last drop of strength I had, I yelled, 'Stop! Chloe, *sto*—'

'Robin, no! You mustn't!'

It was him. Head nodding, eyebrows working, hair flying up and down, he blocked our way with arms jangling like a puppet's.

Rage surged through me. '*Not now, Davey!*' I shouted. 'For goodness' sake, can't you see…'

I stopped.

He wasn't looking at me.

Chloe stood still. Under my touch, her arm still trembled, but it was different, as if a great wave rushed through her. Her lips parted and a smile spread across her face, bringing out the contours of her cheeks and making her eyes glisten. 'Davey?' she whispered.

His arms fell by his sides. The nodding slowed down. He looked up into the radiant face bent to his, an expression dawning in his eyes that I'd never seen before.

I stopped breathing. My hands slid from Chloe's arm. I stood, too close to her to balance properly, yet not daring to move away, in case… in case… what? A longing swept through me. I wrapped my arms around my chest as if that way I could hold on to that precious thing inside; the feeling that pierced me as I watched Chloe kneel down, at eye level with Davey.

'Davey,' she said, over and over. 'You see? I've been here all the time. All these years.'

'Robin.' A slow, shy smile spread across his face. 'Is it really you? Really, really?'

'Really, really,' she echoed, and from the way she spoke, I knew it was an old game between them.

One he'd never played with me.

Chloe rose to her feet. 'You don't have to wait anymore,' she said. 'Come.' She held out her hand.

I just stopped myself from crying out. As if he could take it! But then she seemed to realise, because she dropped her hand, fixing him instead with her gaze as she moved up the slope towards the cedar. He followed – as far as I could tell, because there was something odd about his outline. It began to shimmer.

'Cracked. Completely,' murmured Doug as Chloe passed.

'Um-hm.' Greg nodded.

Dr Rake lurched forwards. 'Don't just stand there,' he commanded. 'Stop the patient! She's getting—'

'No.' Mrs Fielding spoke sharply. 'Leave her alone.'

Her eyes followed Chloe as she reached the group of girls by the cedar. Open-mouthed, Susanna, Lorna and the others fell back, leaving the way clear for Chloe to go by, head turned to the side, a smile on her lips.

'Who's she talking to?' whispered Nina.

I narrowed my gaze. The light must be too bright. Shading my eyes with my hand, I strained to focus on the slight shape walking next to Chloe; now barely more than a movement in the air beside her.

Lucy gave a little squeal and pointed. 'Look!'

Like a breeze stirring the wildflowers. Buttercups, daisies and clover bent and sprang up under invisible footsteps.

Without a word, we followed. Passing the cedar, Chloe carried on along the length of the chapel and, seeing where she was heading, I felt tears prick my eyes.

The gravestone. Where Dr Rake had stood with Chloe. It could only belong to one person.

A great trembling took over my body. I forced my legs onwards, stumbling over the grass, aware of nothing and no one but Chloe – now a solitary figure – coming to a halt and turning, her face lit up.

As I caught up with her, she said, 'He's saying goodbye.'

'Where?'

She nodded to the grass beside the gravestone. 'There. He's just there.'

I shook my head. 'I can't see him.'

She took my bandaged hand gently in hers. 'Then it's working, isn't it? You can still say goodbye.'

The tears swam in my eyes, spilling over, blurring the words carved on the grey stone.

David Alexander Fielding
1937 – 1946
RIP, Little Sparrow

'Goodbye, Davey,' I whispered.

Chloe squeezed my fingertips. 'He's smiling at you,' she said.

Epilogue

'Lucy, you are a genius.'

Three days later and I was still hugging her. Which interfered no end with packing our bags for half-term.

'Honestly, Eleanor' – extracting herself, Lucy rolled her eyes, the pink flush spreading across her face clashing with her bright red curls – 'it was a piece of luck.'

'No, it wasn't. You thought about it. None of the rest of us did.'

'To be fair,' said Lorna, scooping an armful of clothes into the small suitcase on her bed, 'we were all quite busy at the time.'

'Yeah.' Closing the lid of her case, Susanna sat on it and pressed the clasps shut. 'And I'd like to see that toad forcing Chloe into his car with us all around, even if he *had* been able to wave that stupid Emergency Order at everybody.'

'His face!' I stopped stuffing clothes and shoes into my zip bag to savour the glorious memory. 'When he'd searched everywhere and couldn't find it!'

'That'll teach him to leave his briefcase in an unlocked car,' said Lucy, 'which just happened to be on our way to the classroom.'

'Pity you didn't let the air out of his tyres while you were at it,' said Lorna. 'And throw mud at the windscreen.'

'Well, I would've done.' Lucy grinned. 'I was just in a tiny bit of a hurry at the time.'

'Are you girls still packing?' Stalkie appeared in the doorway, bell in hand. 'Everyone else is down at breakfast.'

I'd have to finish later. Might keep Mum and Dad waiting a little, that was all. My spirits soared as I imagined the battered green Mini trundling down the drive, Mum chiding Dad every time he slowed down to look at some architectural detail, Robbie lolling in the back...

Robbie.

In the doorway, I turned round. 'You go,' I said to the others. 'I'll catch you up.'

Hurrying across the dorm, I reached my dressing gown hanging on the opposite door and plunged my hand into the pocket. There, where he'd been since the night of the One-Legged Huntsman, lay Loki. Lifting him out, I stroked his hair as I carried him over to the bag on my bed. 'You can go home now, Loki,' I whispered. 'I don't need you anymore.'

'Eleanor.'

I looked up. Chloe stood at the door. Still thin, yet the cream linen dress she wore didn't hang off her as it would have done a week ago. Her chestnut hair was brushed back from her face, which shone in a way I'd never seen before.

'Chloe, you look great!' I said.

She smiled and walked into the room. 'I've come to say goodbye.'

'We're not going yet,' I said. 'Pickup time is this afternoon.'

'No, *I'm* leaving. Straight after breakfast. A taxi's coming to fetch me.'

My legs gave way. I sat down hard on the bed, crumpling a book and bending the bristles of my hairbrush, bouncing Loki from the top of the zip bag into a corner. None of that mattered. Nothing mattered anymore. Not when Davey had gone and Dr Rake had been chased away and it had all been for nothing.

Quick steps through the room. A swish of skirts, and then hands holding my arms, Chloe's face looking into mine. 'Don't you see? I *can* go now. No one's keeping me here and no one's sending me away. I'm free.'

I blinked. 'So where…?'

'To London. To the Royal College.' Her eyes sparkled. 'I rang them up and – Mother was right – they remembered me. They want me to start at once!'

'Chloe, that's…' I couldn't finish. A bubbling in my chest jumbled every happy word I could think of before it reached my lips. I could only look into her face and grin.

'I want you to have something.' Taking my hands, she pulled me to my feet. Reaching to the wall above the chest of drawers, she removed the painting and held it out. 'For you.'

I looked from the tiny purple chequerboard of the fritillaries in the blue jug to Chloe, smiling and happy in the morning sunlight, and saw, beyond it all, a young boy's face under a cloud of fair hair, blue eyes lighting up as they looked back into mine.

Wrapping my arms around the picture, I pressed it to my heart.

 Matador

For exclusive discounts on Matador titles,
sign up to our occasional newsletter at
troubador.co.uk/bookshop